DOMINION-427

SHADOW OF THE DOMINION, BOOK 4

BLAZE WARD

KNOTTED ROAD PRESS

Dominion-427
Shadow of the Dominion: Book 4
Blaze Ward
Copyright © 2019 Blaze Ward
All rights reserved
Published by Knotted Road Press
www.KnottedRoadPress.com

ISBN: 978-1-64470-090-7

Cover art:
ID 40375662 © Luca Oleastri | Dreamstime.com

Cover and interior design
copyright © 2019 Knotted Road Press

Never miss a release!
If you'd like to be notified of new releases, sign up for my newsletter.

I will never spam you, or use your email for nefarious purposes. You can also unsubscribe at any time.

http://www.blazeward.com/newsletter/

Shadow of the Dominion

Longshot Hypothesis

Hard Bargain

Outermost

Dominion-427

Phoenix

Princess Rualoh

The Jessica Keller Chronicles

Auberon

Queen of the Pirates

Last of the Immortals

Goddess of War

Flight of the Blackbird

The Red Admiral

St. Legier

Winterhome

Petron

CS-405

Queen Anne's Revenge

Packmule

Persephone

Additional Alexandria Station Stories

The Story Road
Siren
Two Bottles of Wine with a War God

The Science Officer Series
The Science Officer
The Mind Field
The Gilded Cage
The Pleasure Dome
The Doomsday Vault
The Last Flagship
The Hammerfield Gambit
The Hammerfield Payoff

Earth Force Sky Patrol
Birth of the Star Dragon
Flight of the Star Dragon
Call of the Star Dragon
Shadow of the Star Dragon
Trial of the Star Dragon

Other Science Fiction Stories
Myrmidons
Moonshot
Menelaus

Earthquake Gun
Moscow Gold

Fairchild

White Crane

The Collective Universe
The Shipwrecked Mermaid

Imposters

[1]

ATHANASIA

"You are sure of these coordinates?" Athanasia demanded as she leaned over the pilot's shoulder to study his screen.

The bridge of *Dominion-427* was a sterile place, painted in off-white walls to dull the mind, along with taupe carpet. The crew's uniforms were equally dreary. Only Athanasia wore anything interesting, dressed in the tight, black leggings and tunic she had chosen for herself on this mission. Her blond hair was up in a single braid today.

Around her buzzed bureaucrats in gray or sage.

She had chased the Anuradhan cargo transport known as *Longshot Hypothesis* for what felt like the width of the galaxy. Out of the Dominion itself. Across all of Laurentia. Even to the far side of the unruly region known as Wildspace, where an ancient, Urlan Empire had apparently been destroyed some two thousand years go.

She was not about to lose that ship now. Too much was riding on her vengeance.

1

"Three degrees north of the southern pole," the captain replied. "Seventeen degrees west of Standard Mean. Those were the coordinates we received from the people at Meeredge."

Athanasia could find no emotions at all in the man's voice as he spoke. It was the only reason she had chosen to fly aboard the Assault Courier *Dominion-427* as long as she had. The man commanding the vessel she had been given by the Dominion authorities was normally so faceless, so utterly anonymous, that she frequently forgot what he looked like if he wasn't standing directly in front of her. Most of the crew was like that, or perhaps she had just never bothered to actually look at any of them as anything more than organic robots.

She kept her curses and growls inside for now. This crew had already carried her far beyond the normal limits of their orders. Abusing them now would just cause most of them to rethink remaining with her when she took her next step. And that was coming soon.

Purchasing another warship, hiring a crew for it to replace the ones that would not choose to accompany her, and turning herself into a warlord of the unruly reaches.

"And the scans of the ground?" she demanded of this captain and his crew, just to be sure.

"Interestingly, we find evidence of a number of atmospheric craft at low elevations or on the ground," the captain spoke carefully, almost thoughtfully. "If I were to attribute purpose to them, I would call the current layout a search pattern by several, distinct groups."

"But no *Longshot Hypothesis*?" she confirmed,

studying the man who was starting to emerge from his colorless shell after so long.

He had even offered her a personal opinion without being required to.

"No spacecraft are present," the captain said. "We even triggered a special signal that should have tripped a standard identifying beacon, just in case. Nothing replied within this quarter of the planetary surface."

Athanasia stepped back from the pilot's shoulder. It did not improve her humor when the man visibly relaxed, but this entire crew was aware that she had once been high in the personal Household of the Dominator himself. She frightened them, as she frequently intended.

"How long will it take to scan the entire surface, if there are so few ships that we might need to investigate?" she asked, trying to inject a note of warmth and detachment from her hostility.

"Three to four days," the man replied, giving her a slight bow from the waist, as if the order were already given and he was just about to execute it.

"Very well, Captain," she said, stepping back again, so that she was a more proper distance away from where her emotions had carried her. "You may proceed."

Athanasia started to turn away, but the man's voice shocked her into halting and turning back.

"What if we do not locate them, in near orbit or on the ground?" he asked in a tone equally suited to discussing the weather.

Athanasia was not fooled, however.

"Then we will locate the nearest industrial system," she said, watching other heads cock in her direction to listen to her words. "Where we will begin the process of dividing the crew."

"Dividing?"

"Some may choose to continue with me, Captain," Athanasia centered her charm on the man. Not because she expected him to be one of them, but so he would convey her mission correctly to his masters when he finally returned home. "I will send the remainder and *Dominion-427* home as soon as I have located and purchased a warship capable of carrying me to my vengeance and destroying Dave Hall and his friends."

Again the bow. Deeper this time. Might this man choose the life of a pirate, over that of a faceless bureaucrat transporting senior politicians around space? She would have doubted it even yesterday, but there was a gleam in his eyes today that left her with doubts.

Athanasia departed the bridge. They would do their duty, especially with the possibility that the hounds had either run their fox to ground, or their mission would change shortly. Many would go home, but she suspected that some would choose to go rogue with her. Piracy was always a tempting alternative to mindless duty.

In her cabin, Stephaneria waited, vibrating with pent-up energy. Athanasia had dressed the woman also in black, showing off the lean, whipcord muscles of the middle-aged, ex-librarian, as opposed to the stout muscles of a woman who had been in the Dominion Household.

Athanasia took Stephaneria's hand and pulled the woman into a hot kiss, just to feel something warm inside herself again. Too many years without any touch from the man she had married nearly three decades ago.

Athanasia could never return to the Dominion. Anyone with half a brain could calculate that easily enough. The old Dominator had been assassinated by a man who subsequently escaped justice. The new Dominator had been crowned by now, although it might take years for the news to cross Wildspace to reach her. Whoever it was would not welcome the widow of the former Dominator. She would be shuffled off to a retirement pension, well away from Cronus Prime and the center of power. Perhaps they would just have her killed. It didn't matter, she was never returning to inquire.

She had to chase down a man who called himself Dave Hall these days, and kill the bastard. Once, he had been her husband, when he'd had another name. Before he assassinated the Dominator and fled into the darkness, one step ahead of the Dominion's Internal Security Bureau, the White Hats, who had also betrayed her.

Athanasia could not tell anyone on this ship the truth, except for things she might whisper in Stephaneria's ear as they cuddled at night, sweaty and sated.

Dave Hall hadn't just been the assassin.

He had been the Dominator himself.

[2]

DAVE

DAVE SMILED as he looked around the compact bridge, really just a cockpit for two pilots, and considered everything. His original goal had been to fly with Valentinian for six months or so, just to keep a low enough profile that nobody would come looking for him.

After that, disappear around a corridor curve at a station and vanish from the knowledge of men. Use one of the other identities he had created, and all the cash, and live a quiet life somewhere.

Hadn't worked.

Oh, he had maneuvered the situation expertly. Valentinian's former first mate found a better job, working as part owner of a bar on Tuska Station. That left a spot open where Dave had planned to slip into. That part even worked, more or less.

Right up until the White Hats had decided something didn't add up, and unraveled his scheme in days, when it should have taken them years.

A noise behind him caused Dave to glance back

over his left shoulder. He smiled at Kyriaki as she brought him some coffee.

"What's so funny?" she asked as she handed him a fresh bulb and took the empty one from the cup holder in the console.

"Wondering where Vee and I would be today, if you weren't so damned relentless," he said.

"He'd probably have gotten himself killed by Nash," Kyriaki's face soured almost enough to wipe the grin from his. "You'd have ended up selling *Longshot* and walking away. Dave Hall would be dead now, too, and the world would be a darker place."

Dave couldn't remember a time when she had sounded like a poet. Kyriaki was a cop. Ex-cop, anyway. The very White Hat that decided the story smelled wrong and tugged on threads until something came loose.

Who had let him go, after he had helped her rescue Vee on Tartarus, when she could have taken him back to Cronus Prime in chains and been considered the greatest agent in the history of the Dominion.

He occasionally wondered if she had regrets, giving up that other life to become part of their crew. Later, she had known too much, and the Dominion would have put her under truth serum to get the whole story, so she'd have been killed as well.

He turned far enough to really study her face. Something had changed, right before they left Kryuome to escape the Widow.

Kyriaki Apokapes was both more relaxed, and more tense than she had been.

Dave hadn't asked. He might be old enough to be

her father, but the group of them had all been partners in this, including Bayjy and the Mondi warrior-pilot Glaxu.

"I feel like I should get you and Vee drunk," Dave offered in a low voice. "Strip you both naked and throw you into one of the empty cabins upstairs and let you two work it all out."

There was a distinct flash of emotion in her eyes. To Dave, it somehow combined anger, lust, and fear. Like she wanted to, but was afraid to actually take that step.

He'd seen the two of them. Valentinian and Kyriaki. Every once in a while, they'd suddenly be standing too close, almost dancing except that they weren't touching. Carefully *not touching*, but they wanted to.

Binary stars orbiting a common center, wondering who might kiss the other first. Or punch.

Two hard-headed, stubborn kids. Dave could say that. His own children were about the same age. He'd gotten all that silliness out of his system decades ago. At least he hoped so.

Most women looked at him and saw a huge bruiser of a man. Nearly a head taller than Vee. Not brutally ugly, like some of his old Caelon troopers, but not the sort of pirate bad-boy that walked into a room and carbonated the hormones of every woman present, like Vee seemed to do.

Kyriaki started to say something and paused. A second time. A third.

"What the hell happened back there?" Dave asked. "I have never seen you like this."

"It got complicated," she whispered.

Dave couldn't help himself. He started laughing.

If the bulb hadn't been sealed, he probably would have spilled coffee down his front and all over his lap.

She looked like she was measuring him for a punch, but something broke in her a few seconds later and she joined him in giggling.

"Sorry," he finally gasped. "*Got* complicated."

She finally grinned at him with her mouth pulled sideways in a way that reminded Dave of his daughter Euphrosyne.

"Yeah, I suppose so," Kyriaki breathed out and let a little color into her voice. "We were almost there. Talking serious stuff. And then the damned Widow had to show up and kinda ruin everything."

"Delay, perhaps," Dave nodded. "Not ruin. We're still a team. Still free and in motion. We'll get to Chatosig and wait her out. We've got enough money on hand that we won't go broke anytime soon. The rest is just patience."

"Patience. Right," she said in a sarcastic tone. "Not sure I want patience."

"He'll come around, Kyriaki," Dave replied in a much calmer voice. "You frighten him even more than you do me, and that's saying something. Give him time."

"How much?" she asked, pain evident now.

Dave shrugged.

"If he hadn't been a hard, stubborn, brilliant con artist with an ethical streak and the luck of the gods on his side, I wouldn't have picked him in the first place," Dave nodded. "And like you said, we'd be dead now, most likely. He'll come around."

"I hope so," Kyriaki muttered.

Dave let her go as she turned away. Stared out at

the lines of warpspace outside the little bubble universe that was *Longshot Hypothesis* and considered the lines in his past and future like those stars out there around him.

Valentinian's luck had carried them all this far, through Dominion security and crooked poker games, to Wildspace planets with radioactive ruins hiding treasure. Chatosig would be the next phase of the grand adventure, then hopefully they could finally escape his ex-wife and live a peaceful life.

Not that he believed it for a minute.

[3]

GLAXU

HE CONSIDERED BEING MORTALLY OFFENDED as he studied the readout displayed before him, but Glaxu had known that forming a Southern Chain with the human ship *Longshot Hypothesis* threatened to upend his understanding of speed.

At least once Captain Tarasicodissa had explained to him how fast that vessel really was.

Based on the elapsed travel time, Glaxu wondered for the eighth or tenth time if the cargo ship was pulling him through warpspace, rather than Glaxu's Mondi fightership *Outermost* pushing. And that was a cargo transport?

Glaxu left the cockpit of his craft and headed aft to the Larder. Past the Cactus, the room where he slept, and the Branch, where he pooped compact turds recycled for carbon.

What he really wanted right now was something that affected a Mondi like alcohol did to humans. A nice, pleasant poisoning that left few aftereffects and introduced a calmness and relaxation. There were certain plants back home that one chewed for trace alkaloids that would produce an equivalent sensation. Apparently humans did something similar, but they would try anything at least once. Even things that might kill them.

After a few weeks with Captain Tarasicodissa and his other crew, Glaxu no longer wondered how humans had managed to completely overrun this sector of the galaxy and fill in all the ecological niches once filled by Urlan or other species.

That fool back on Kryuome, the human warlord names Truqtok, had learned at great personal expense just how dangerous those four humans were. He could include Bayjy in there, even if she was Pranai. That just meant she was a Variant Human. Tall and well-muscled. Light purple as a base color, rather than the pink/brown of the others. Human in all the external ways.

She, at least, liked proper temperatures, above forty degrees Centigrade, rather than the much colder temperatures that the captain kept his ship, most of the time.

Glaxu fixed himself a bowl of juice and tipped it slowly back into his beak.

Mondi normally got all of their fluid intake from their food, but Glaxu and his previous nest had spent enough time in human-dominated space to develop the habit of drinking liquid refreshment from a shallow bowl, in this case by pouring it with both stubby hands, rather than using his long tongue to lap it up.

Just another mark of how far from his home nest he had traveled.

But this nest, Captain Tarasicodissa and the

others, Kyriaki Apokapes, Bayjy Endon, and not-Dave Hall, had shown themselves to be extremely resourceful, and far more dangerous than Glaxu would have believed from such a small team of humans. And they had accepted him, a small land bird that not-Dave Hall had once called a *Dire Ground Cuckoo* when he didn't think Glaxu was around.

Better than the normal human pejorative, which was to call him a roadrunner. Apparently some worlds had a similar creature, unintelligent and much smaller, but following the same basic design patterns. Except they didn't fight with a dewclaw capable of opening a silly human up like a knife through butter.

Glaxu grinned and returned the bowl to the shelf. He would check the flight path of this new Southern Chain one last time before sleeping for a few hours.

Yes, a speed his old nest could not have matched on their best day, just emerging from the tuning nests back home. Perhaps he needed to convince his friends to visit his own homeworld after this next set of adventures, to show his kin that he wasn't a screw-up after all. Merely the one they had correctly nicknamed *Farther*. Perhaps *Farthest* would be even more appropriate, if he introduced the great nest to these killers, and had Captain Tarasicodissa show the Mondi how to build properly fast engines.

Mondi didn't need to conquer the galaxy, but it would be nice to be able to stop the humans, when that species finally came to Mondi sectors to try.

"STAND by to come out of warpbubble," Valentinian glanced over at Dave and made sure the Big Guy was paying attention.

They had tried the Southern Chain thing with *Outermost,* just to prove it worked, but that had only been for a few minutes the first time. Technological compatibility. Reshaping the overall warpbubble itself to be less round and more arrow shaped.

Longshot Hypothesis had taken to that like a duck to water. Or a shark to fresh chum.

Valentinian decided he was going to have to start lying to people about departure dates, or run his Overdrive engines at maybe half-power, if Glaxu stayed with them for long. They were already thirty-three hours ahead of the estimated normal transit time listed in the Gazetteer for a path between Kryuome and Chatosig.

Great if you needed to get priority cargo or fresh fruit between two points. Lousy if the pirates of this galaxy discovered just how fast he was and decided they needed to try to take the ship away from him.

Of course, his oversized armory might come in handy at that point. Most ships in the trade carried only a handful of weapons. Flamers, pain pistols, maybe a plasma rifle.

Valentinian was up to two hundred and forty-three weapons of one sort or another in there. Probably time to start selling some off again, or trade the crap he kept getting after winning bar fights for a couple of really expensive pieces. This was Wildspace. What sorts of silliness could he buy, with money burning a hole in his pocket?

Dave nodded to him as the clock on the central control board counted down. Hopefully, Glaxu was paying attention and would be able to shut down his own systems on time, so they didn't end up too far separated when they came out at the outer buoys of the Chatosig system. They could get organized and sail down to one of the stations in tandem, just in case anybody got frisky.

Longshot Hypothesis was unarmed and unarmored. At present. Valentinian had plans to add a bubble turret on top of the ship, but hadn't ever had the cash. Or the need. Or the time.

That might be changing.

For now, he had *Outermost*, a Mondi variable-geometry slayership with one small cannon on the centerline and two bigger ones on the wings, moving around as the ship changed shape and assault profile. Not a bad thing to have flying as a consort.

"Dropping to zero in four, three, two, one, mark," Dave called the cadence.

Longshot Hypothesis brought itself out of the

warpbubble a little shy of the outer markers, but that was by design. Valentinian wanted time to get organized.

Chatosig, down below them in the gravity fields, was a pleasant-enough planet, according to the Gazette. Exported foodstuffs and raw minerals up to a ring of orbital facilities, about a third of which were pure zero-g factories, where you could do strange things in the manufacturing process.

The other two-thirds were standard stations. Factories making things. A couple of shipyards building and repairing things, although the notes said the city of Soko, down on the surface, was home to a half-dozen shipyards capable of building things clear up to the medium freighter scale. Or perhaps a Dominion Assault Courier, like the one that had already chased them clear across space to Kryuome.

At least Bayjy had been here before, so she knew the lay of the land, hopefully. Valentinian wouldn't know anyone, so scoring a cargo to haul around would be difficult, and probably end up not making him anything, with the thin margins he would have to charge to get someone to take a chance on the newcomer.

But he really wasn't here for merchant stuff. Bayjy had been a salvager in her previous life before coming aboard. And he had a treasure map that had led him to a spot on the surface of Kryuome, right before *Dominion-427* had showed up and chased them off.

Hopefully, there was something down on Kryuome that they could open, loot, and sell on the open market for a lot of money.

Because right before all hell had broken loose, he

and Kyriaki had been talking about the future. Once upon a time, Valentinian had figured that in another ten years, if he was careful, he'd have enough money salted away to retire to a careful life of leisure. That or buy more ships and turn himself into a corporate power. Ick, but better than starving, that was for sure.

A life of legitimate business was out of the question now, at least back in the Dominion or Laurentia. He'd need to keep most of Wildspace between him and everyone's past, at least for several more years. Maybe forever, depending.

But he'd get there. Falling into shit and coming out smelling like a rose was his superpower, it seemed.

"*Outermost*, this is *Longshot Hypothesis*," Valentinian said into the microphone as the scanners got organized and started to feed them information about this new system.

"Ready for engagement, Leader," Glaxu's cheerful voice came back.

The compact birdman always seemed ready to kill things, especially when he was in that tiny warship. And Valentinian would also have Dave and Kyriaki, armed to the teeth and backing him up. Or maybe the three of them were the goons, four with Glaxu, and Bayjy was the merchant on this run.

The galaxy had gotten weird again, but he could still out-think, out-gun, or out-run whoever he encountered. He had come too far to give up now.

[5]
BAYJY

SHE WASN'T GOING to jinx it as she walked around the concourse of the station and say it was good to be home, but Chatosig was at least someplace she had passed through a few times, and it felt closer to that mythological home that the Pranai didn't have. Her kind were from space, no two ways about it.

The Urlan had cut loose with their megalomania and god-complex shit and created all manner of servant species. Humans apparently bred the best, and were the most successful, so now there were all sorts of Variants out there who didn't have a homeworld, just a station or ship that they had been born on.

She felt at home here anyway, even if she wouldn't go so far as to tell Captain or Big Guy that. Kyrie was safe enough, maybe.

Station hadn't changed. That was one of the most reliable things in space. Planets had seasons and stuff. Stations were cast in steel and patience, kinda like her. People might come and go. Shops would change owners and theme, but the bones were always there.

They were here today.

This space had been a chandlery, last time she was here, maybe a year and a half ago. The restaurant on the right side had expanded and taken it over, so hopefully they were doing well. She had walked this way because the old shop had always been a great place to pick up semi-junk that a Senior Cutter salvager chick like her could frequently repair.

Old woman who ran the joint must not have been making enough money. Or maybe had just moved on.

We all move on.

Table for four, plus a booster pillar for Glaxu, so he could squat at table level with everyone and belong. Place had to serve a lot of aliens if they had that many options available.

Waitress took drink orders and left menus. Not much in the way of fresh greens. Lots of things that came out of a freezer and got quick-warmed by an autochef. Reliable, however mundane. You'd get the same food the galaxy over.

Idly, Bayjy wondered if anyone had created a silent chain of such restaurants. *We'll provide the food from this list of stuff. You buy it in bulk and the boxes include the recipe programs for your autochefs to cook it.*

She could see that turning into a form of comfort food. Any station you went to, you could get that one thing you grew up on.

She needed a little comfort food right now. They had been so close, back on Kryuome. Big Guy had just started to build a hunk of metal he called a key, and then Captain said bug out and run.

Stupid Widow. Man don't want you, why are you chasing his ass all the way across the galaxy? Get on with your life.

'Course, based on Kyrie's stories, the woman would do exactly that, once she had Big Guy's head on a stake. And Captain's. And Kyrie's.

Probably need to add hers and Glaxu's, just 'cause at that point. That made it kinda personal.

Bayjy sighed quietly and studied the menu. It hadn't changed in decades, near as she could tell. Chain restaurant kind of food, they just didn't tell anybody that.

"What's good?" Kyrie asked.

"It's station food," Bayjy looked up at her.

And sighed again. *You people really have never been out in the galaxy and poor, have you?*

"Buy it by the ton," Bayjy continued. "Run it through the autochef onto a plate. Carbs, protein, maybe some nutrition if you're lucky. Should even feed Glaxu, although we'll have to find someplace else if he wants fresh snake more than once in a blue moon."

It struck her then what relative poverty tasted like. The Dominion was a rich place. And Big Guy had been at the top of the pyramid. Kyrie had been a cop on the capital station, so she had eaten well her whole life. Only Captain probably understood, and he was still a way-outsider here, feeling his way along by luck.

Bayjy set her menu down and pointed at a couple of things for Kyrie.

"You'll probably like these well enough," Bayjy said simply. "I'm getting this one. Glaxu, you should stay with one of these."

After a moment, everyone nodded and it hit her that they were going to take her suggestions at face value. No arguing. No whining. Assume she was right and that was that.

Damn it, she'd been with Butler and his crew of lunkheads for too long.

Waitress seemed to sense that the moment had come and returned. Orders got placed. An appetizer was thrown in, mostly on the off-chance that the greens in it had been flash-frozen at some point and still had some nutritional value.

Bayjy sighed again.

"Not giving up my armory," Captain said quietly.

"I know," Bayjy surrendered quietly. "But fresh veggies would be a nice treat."

"Not giving up my cabins, either," Valentinian went on. "Might actually have paying customers at some point."

"If we had the time, we could maybe stretch the wings and add a room or two," Big Guy chimed in.

Like they hadn't discussed this to death already.

Kyrie suddenly got a wicked gleam in her eyes. The dangerous kind. Ex-cop-gone-totally-rogue-killer-babe kind.

"So we need to add a winch to the truck," she said, completely off-topic in all the best ways. "And a crane arm or something, so we can lift heavy stuff, right?"

Heads nodded. Another discussion for late nights with mildly alcoholic stimulation.

"And we need to get an overhead crane for the cargo bay as well, right?" the blond chick went on.

Captain suddenly sat up a little straighter. Bayjy did, too. Big Guy was too busy being tough.

"We ever going to haul Anuradhan cargo boxes again?" Kyrie turned to Valentinian with the most innocent face Bayjy could remember from her. "Ten meters wide. Ten tall. Thirty long?"

"I would be utterly surprised if they even existed out here in those dimensions," Captain breathed a little heavy, rather than actually spoke. Like maybe he could see where she was going.

"Still, we might have enough clearance anyway," Kyrie supplied with a guileless smile. "Build out a frame overhead on I-beams. Either put the winch on it, or just run a pulley out like a tongue. That ought to give you a little more than two and a half meters of clearance you could enclose on the top side of those beams, depending on how thick you wanted your decks. More storage, maybe, if you ran an extension from the top of the staircase, like an attic. Or maybe a greenhouse. Whole other deck, if you wanted to move crew back there and free up your two cabins forward for paying customers."

Bayjy had forgotten to breathe. Her lungs started bitching at her, so she came back to the present and listened to the others start breathing as well. *Kinda catching, ya know?*

Doing something like that would mean a commitment from Captain that the two of them were more than just temporary contractors. More than seasonal crew.

Family, maybe, weird as they all looked together.

Appetizer arrived like a meteor striking the surface of a planet. Everything went squish emotionally and kinda splattered everywhere. Bayjy wasn't sure that the mud was ever getting washed out. Captain's face was as unreadable as she'd ever seen it at a poker table, but that was probably a good thing.

Meant he was calculating all the odds, which took a while when playing Arcades.

Bayjy snatched a pastry puff before anyone else recovered enough to deny her. There were eleven, so somebody was getting three. Might as well be her.

Psychological warfare on the Captain sure worked up a pretty good appetite in a girl.

[6]
ATHANASIA

Walking onto the bridge of *Dominion-427* almost felt like returning to the scene of a crime at this point. Athanasia had already moved past this ship and this crew, just in the five days that they had been sitting in a high orbit.

Eleven ships had arrived or departed in that time. With so little orbital traffic, her ship had inspected each and every one of them at least from a polite distance. About half had appeared to have been armed.

Hard Bargain had finally shown up two days ago. Captain Butler Vidy-Wooders claimed that to be the best speed he could make across the intervening distance. If so, Athanasia was even less impressed with the M'Rai.

She suspected he had been too drunk to make the original departure time, and lied to cover it up later. Word had gotten out about the captain, at least at the stations Valentinian Tarasicodissa had hit so far. From there it would ripple outward in waves as other captains told their friends the latest gossip. How the captain of the salvager *Hard Bargain* had dumped his crew rather than pay them their share of a major haul. How one of them had gotten back at the man in the most embarrassing way possible.

No credible professionals would ever hire on with him again. He might as well just sell his ship and take a job planetside, once enough people knew the truth.

Or he could hire on to pilot the pirate warship Athanasia had purchased. She would just need to make sure that the crew remained loyal to her, and not to him. With his reputation, that wouldn't be nearly as difficult as it might have been before.

The Captain of *Dominion-427* rose from his seat as she entered. He had changed from the bland bureaucrat who had been ordered to transport her to wherever would get the Widow away from the halls of power. Something had come alive in the man. Or perhaps he had finally decided to allow Athanasia to see the inner man.

She had spent twenty-five years in the Dominion Household. Every meal had been taken while wearing a half-mask to hide their faces. All of the Household had been like that. Much of the top of the Solar Party that actually ruled the Dominion as well.

Even there the Dominator, her former husband, only gave orders. Set policy. But the bureaucrats did the work. Men and women who worked extremely diligently to be masks themselves.

What did it mean that Captain Iulianus Palaiologos was suddenly turning into a person around her? Was he planning to remain behind when his ship went home? Or had he concluded that she no longer mattered as a power to be assuaged, and could stop playing such games?

Briefly, as she approached, Athanasia wondered if he might be worth taking to bed once, just to find out. Stephaneria was lovely, unfurling like a morning flower under Athanasia's touch and guidance. But occasionally Athanasia would have liked a male.

Butler Vidy-Wooders had been on that list of possible...yes, she should call them victims if she was being honest with herself. The Variant Humanity known as M'Rai, two and a half to three meters tall, were apparently still designed to mate with humans of a normal scale. In a way, that was perhaps the greatest shame, but Athanasia would have made something work.

But perhaps Captain Palaiologos should be on her list as well?

"What news?" she asked as she came to rest the slightest shade closer to the man than she had before.

He noticed. The man was highly observant of these things. It had just never appeared in his eyes before now.

"It is my opinion that *Longshot Hypothesis* was here," the captain replied, even including a touch of color to his voice. "Their claims to be excavating the southern polar region were likely a ruse to mislead the locals, while they went elsewhere."

"How did they escape us?" Athanasia inquired.

"I think they spotted us on arrival," Palaiologos said. "We pinged the planet before we realized that there was no central authority to contact. They heard, waited for us to land, and then likely fled when we first touched, or perhaps while we made our way to the city known as Meeredge. Two days elapsed there.

If they were careful, and remained below our scanner horizon during that time, it would have worked. That is how I would have done it, in their shoes."

Athanasia barely controlled the blink that wanted to shutter her eyes. She had only once heard the man offer a personal opinion without being ordered to first before this.

"Will they return?" Athanasia asked.

She nearly fainted with shock when the man simply shrugged and made a tilted-head frogface at her. It was like he was actually human underneath that mask he had probably worn his entire life.

But then, who was she to argue? Where was the utterly-self-contained woman who had once been married to the Dominator? She had taken off that entire identity like a suit of old clothes when she remade herself into the Widow. Had taken Stephaneria as a consort and apprentice and lover.

Had become a destroyer intent on carving out her own empire from the worlds of Wildspace.

For a moment, Athanasia considered if she should simply let Dave Hall go. He would never return to her, just as he would never again be the Dominator. Was her time better spent building her power now? She could always hire assassins to go after the man from there. If she owned a chunk of Wildspace, he would either have to cross out of the human zones entirely, or flee back towards places like Asherah or Qetesh. Neither him nor his captain would ever be able to hide in Lei-Ze, so that wasn't an option.

Should she be free?

That was too much to calculate for today. But tomorrow?

"Get me *Hard Bargain* on the screen," Athanasia announced.

On another Dominion vessel, that should have been a matter of seconds. It took nearly three minutes before the man's ugly face appeared on the screen.

"Yeah?" he half-growled.

Athanasia wondered if he had been asleep. The eyes were too focused for him to be more than mildly drunk right now.

"Where would they go from here?" she asked. "Tarasicodissa is no longer in this system."

More thinking, as if it was a foreign concept, or perhaps a disease he needed to fight off at every opportunity.

"Poekangibed is closest," he finally muttered. "Another poor shithole in space barely worth the trip."

"I want an industrialized system, Captain," Athanasia fixed her ire on the man. "Preferably one known for shipyards."

If there was a way to extract his knowledge of Wildspace and its seedier sides, without the man's ugly personality, she would have already done so.

Athanasia could already see the day she needed to replace this fool with someone else, one equally controllable by his fear, his dick, or his poverty.

"That would be Chatosig. Been there a few times. Endon would know the system."

Vidy-Wooders scratched idly at the side of his face. Athanasia hoped that he didn't have anything living in that unkempt beard.

"Very good, Captain Vidy-Wooders," Athanasia said. "We shall set course to Chatosig immediately. If they have ships, I will probably buy one there and look to hiring a crew. If you wish to remain with my mission of vengeance at that point, we will talk."

Athanasia turned to her own captain and nodded. One of the crew cut the signal, replacing it on the big screen with the Dominion flag.

"It will be done soon," Athanasia announced in a brighter voice than she had before. "Let everyone know to prepare for the next phases of their lives, whatever choice that entails."

She spoke those last words while focused on Captain Iulianus Palaiologos. If she could keep him, she would have a competent commander. One she could trust. Possibly even one willing to be kept on a leash. Butler Vidy-Wooders was fast becoming a bore, with little to recommend him besides a coarse knowledge and low cunning.

Her empire would need people in charge who could tie their own laces without assistance.

[7]
VALENTINIAN

Longshot Hypothesis was oddly designed, compared to most other cargo ships Valentinian had ever encountered. That was part of why he loved her so.

The engines were up on the front of the ship hanging from a pair of wings that stuck out of the ship's front shoulders. Between them were the six cabins, three to a side, plus the two common spaces and the kitchen, at least on the upper deck. His bridge was right below the kitchen on the main deck, forward from the cargo hall aft.

Most ships had the bridge above the main cargo deck, so you could fly yourself right up to the station, nosing bow-in for docking. Made it easier for most crews, who tended to rely on the autopilot for things like that.

You left by carefully backing out of your bay until you had enough space around you, pivoted on gyros and thrusters, and then engaged the engines.

Valentinian didn't know may people who could

back a beast like *Longshot* into a docking port with nothing but rear-facing cameras. That always left him in a spot where he could make a fast getaway, if necessary. Had turned out to be vital on more than one occasion. Undock, light the engines, and push as hard or soft as you needed to get away from someone that had to back out.

And once *Longshot Hypothesis* got the marker buoys, you were never catching her anyway.

This ship had been his home for nearly three years now. His first crew had been Artaxerxes, as the old man taught the hotshot kid how to be a captain. Then Dave Hall came along and made up for his lack of mechanical expertise with size, strength, and lethal brutality.

"Still think it's a good idea?" Dave had snuck up behind him as Valentinian stood in the cargo bay next to the lifter truck they had acquired on Kryuome.

Valentinian knew what Dave was referring to. For a long moment the two of them just looked up at the ceiling.

"I'm torn," Valentinian finally admitted. To himself as well as to his First Mate, and probably his best friend in the galaxy right now. "It changes everything."

He didn't have to explain what everything was. They both knew.

"I would maybe suggest getting a bigger, faster ship, but I don't think such a thing really exists," Dave offered.

"Remember, the guy who sold her to me upgraded, after you finally conquered Anuradha," Valentinian teased. "These hulls were dirt cheap, even with the massive upgrades he had done. Don't know what he was flying with my money, though."

Valentinian glanced over when the giant next to him fell silent. That meant Dave was thinking, rather than just listening. Especially with that look on his face.

"I remember a larger design from my invasion plans," Dave said after a few moments. "Wings twice as thick, front to back, with a second row of cabins up there. Added four total, I think. Longer overall hull but the same shape. Put a third engine up centerline, like the fin on a shark. If he did the same thing to that that he did to this, engine-wise, that would be worth the upgrade. As long as you don't mind being taxed as a medium freighter and not one of the light jobbies."

"Guessing he probably classified it as a personal yacht at that point," Valentinian said. "He struck me as the guy that had made enough money, and pushed his luck far enough, that he was getting out of the business before it caught up with him."

"Understand that concept," Dave laughed quietly. "I did the same thing myself."

"This feels like a lot of commitment," Valentinian said, just as quietly. "I mean, we can do it. Makes sense, gives us more space to work with, and only thing we lose is the ability to stand on top of an Anuradhan cargo box if we ever find one again. If time wasn't an object, nor money, I'd add four rooms and a head up there. Maybe a crew rec room/kitchen thing to go with the greenhouse Bayjy wants to put in. And add a turret aft with a gun of some sort. Pretty sure it would take Kyriaki all of five minutes to master anything we mounted."

"But?" Dave asked.

"How soon is your wife coming after us, Dave?" Valentinian asked. "Way cheaper to do this all at once, rather than adding things in pieces, but that takes us off-line for maybe a month, once they start cutting and welding. Do we risk it here, or run like hell for the farthest place we can find that can do the work right, hoping she won't find us again? I'm already amazed she kept on us this long. It frightens me that she might never stop."

"Plus, Bayjy has friends here, or folks she could ask," Dave nodded. "Anywhere else we go, it becomes a crapshoot. And *Longshot Hypothesis* stands out. Nobody else in the galaxy builds them like that, at least as far as I know. The memory of your ship will stick in minds after we've left. I know gearheads like you."

Valentinian laughed. Not something he could argue with.

"How good are you with a welder?" he asked the former warlord of known space. "One alternative is to buy a lot of sheet metal and bar stock, plus some tools, and do the rough work ourselves, out in space where we can turn the gravity off to move things around. Then it is just a matter of mass."

"I built my telescoping baton," Dave grinned down at him. "I can probably figure out which end of a welder is the hot part, at least on the second try."

"Let's talk to the other three then," Valentinian said. "I'd like to see if we can pick up a cargo when we're buying metal. Maybe we can make this work out."

[8]
BAYJY

"Hello again, pretty lady."

Bayjy looked up surprised from the pile of junk on the table that had caught her eye. She was always surprised that Ozzo was still around. He had to be the oldest human she had ever met, maybe into his second century now and still going like a pup. A wrinkled one, but still a puppy at heart.

"Did not hear that *Hard Bargain* was in town," Ozzo continued with a meaningful look at Captain and Kyrie, trailing along. Big Guy was back on the ship and Glaxu was supposedly taking a nap.

"Not flying with that bastard anymore," Bayjy kinda growled at the shopkeeper.

Couldn't help it. Still a sour spot there.

"Oh?" Ozzo asked as Bayjy companions moved a little to each side and left her at least the illusion of a little privacy.

Ozzo's shop would have probably been pretty roomy if you got all the junk out of it. But you couldn't actually do that short of backing a lifter and a garbage sled up to the front hatch. Some places probably hadn't seen light in decades.

"*Hard Bargain*'s captain, Butler, dumped me and everyone else at a place called Bohrne Station, clear over in Laurentia," Bayjy said. "We had hit a big payday, an Urlan Troop transport with a full chapel intact. He didn't want to pay us our shares, so he gave us leave on a new station to celebrate, backed away, and left us there."

"Bad juju," the tiny ancient nodded with a serious anger in his eyes.

Bayjy felt the man's attention turn to Captain like a spotlight. Saw the appraising look, before it turned to Kyrie.

"Better crew now," he said simply.

It hadn't been a question. Bayjy nodded anyway.

"And we got more treasure to seek," Bayjy smiled at the shopkeeper. "This one's planetside, so I need to augment some of my old tools, and break in some newbies to the fine art of salvage."

"Underground?" Ozzo asked sideways.

"First part of it, yeah," Bayjy agreed. "Had to back away from the dig in a hurry, so don't know more than that."

"Scalpers or competitors?" Ozzo asked, suddenly waving a hand at her. "Come, this is junk. Better stuff hidden in back."

Bayjy glanced at her companions, but they were letting her lead. She was making decisions, rather than having to try to wheedle things out of Butler that she needed.

It was so much better this way. Weirder, but awesomer.

"Closer to scalpers," Bayjy said as she entered the labyrinth of Ozzo's little world. "Complicated."

Shelves stacked floor to ceiling. Mostly junk tools, but occasional gems lost when someone ran out of cash in a hurry. Good pickings, if you were lucky enough to be there the right day.

She glanced back at Captain and he nodded carefully at her, so she continued talking. They were deep enough now that someone walking by outside wouldn't overhear them unless they crossed that same light that made the room beep with customers.

"Dominion folks kinda mad at some of my crewmates," Bayjy explained to Ozzo.

"Angry enough to chase them this far into Wildspace?" Ozzo stopped and turned around, reappraising everyone in a new light, focusing on Captain. "Ex-husband or insurance investigator?"

Bayjy nearly laughed at the outrage that had crossed Kyrie's face for just a moment, at the suggestion that Valentinian had maybe seduced her away from some other man. Not entirely off-base, but that would be even harder to explain.

"Estranged wife, actually," Captain spoke up now. "Not mine, thankfully. First Mate can't get far enough away from the woman, her money, or her power."

"Ah," Ozzo nodded sagely. "That can be a problem. Perhaps your friend should consider fleeing across known space, changing his name, and opening a junk shop on a distant station somewhere."

Bayjy blinked in surprise at the implications of how Ozzo had originally gotten here. The man had been around so long that people probably forgot that he had been young once. Maybe eighty years ago, but still.

"Two of the three, so far," Valentinian laughed. "Not sure we've gone far enough yet."

Ozzo continued to nod to some inner rhythm, like music playing only in his head.

"Here, Pretty Lady," Ozzo put a hand down on a device Bayjy didn't recognize. "You need."

"What is it?" she asked, just touching the casing with one finger.

Round. Disk-shaped, about fifteen centimeters tall and forty-five across. Black metal hull. Looked heavy.

"Ground scanner," Ozzo laughed in a merry song that was almost a bird's tune. "Repulsors float it about a foot above ground. Just smart enough to walk a grid one hundred meters on a side and then return to starting point. It will beep loudly and stop if it encounters life forms, but you won't probably find those anywhere you're working."

"Life forms?" Bayjy was intrigued and appalled at the same time.

"Designed for avalanche rescue," Ozzo grinned. "Or anywhere else people get buried alive suddenly."

"How'd it get here?" she asked, at a loss.

Ozzo shrugged eloquently.

"Stuff makes its way until it stops," the man said, almost quoting some kind of Zen koan. "Then it finds a new purpose and continues. People are same way."

She turned to Captain and got his nod.

Still her game to play.

"How much?" she asked.

Ozzo quoted her a price that was impossibly cheap. Like, less than he could probably get just selling it to a recycler to render the metal down into bars.

"That can't be right," Bayjy felt her argumentative side kick in. "You aren't charging me enough for it."

Ozzo laughed uproariously.

"You make poor merchant, Pretty Lady," he said after he stopped to breathe. "It cost me almost nothing to acquire, has sat here patiently waiting for purpose, and now you arrive. Is good."

"Almost nothing?" Bayjy asked. "This?"

"In my business, we call them estate sales," Ozzo turned serious. "Man dies suddenly. No family. No friends. Stuff left over. Detritus that marks our entire existence on this phase of the wheel. My kind vultures. Swoop in, pick carcass clean. Sell for profit, keep store running."

Bayjy watched the happy, goofy old man suddenly transform before her eyes into someone that Big Guy would have probably walked a wide path around, rather than brush against him accidentally on a station concourse.

"You don't ever own anything that you can't carry with you at a dead run," Ozzo the deadly shopkeeper pronounced. "Keep that in mind."

Bayjy gulped. It was like being threatened by a rabbit, except this one had blood staining the fur around his muzzle and claws coming out of all four feet.

Ozzo grinned and suddenly the elderly shopkeeper was back, smiling at her with bright, expectant eyes.

"You buy?"

"Yeah," Bayjy managed to get her stammer under control before she spoke. Or passed out from shock.

"Lemme look around and see what else you have. Need some generalist gear. All my stuff is tuned for dead spaceships in orbit, with me in a suit."

Ozzo got a still, pensive look on his face. He pointed over one shoulder to the far, back, right-hand corner of the shop.

"You start there and work your way forward along the outer wall," Ozzo said, and then ignored her completely to look over her shoulder at Valentinian.

"Captain, what needs do you bring to my threshold?"

[9]
DAVE

THERE WERE STILL moments when the urge to walk off Vee's deck, turn left, and disappear forever snuck up and bit him on the ass, but Dave worked hard to suppress them.

For one, it wouldn't do him or anyone else any good. He'd burned that bridge a long time ago, pulling Vee into this mess. Kyriaki had not done herself any favors, but even a White Hat can find the spot where law and ethics diverge, and end up making the right choice, however much it might have cost her personally.

If he left, they would still be hunted by the Widow. Athanasia wouldn't give up until she had them all dead. Dave understood that about his estranged wife. Could he finally call her an ex-wife at this point? Common law and all that? Legally abandoned?

Dave didn't know. Didn't really matter. Either they had escaped her by fleeing from Kryuome, or they hadn't. He didn't think she'd stay put looking for him there, but Dave had also warned Vee that they didn't dare stay long here, or on the planet below, until they were sure they had lost the woman for good.

If that was possible.

Longshot Hypothesis stuck in minds. From below, she looked like a hawk pouncing, when most transports he had known were either utilitarian boxes designed to maximize space and minimize atmospheric drag, or brutalist architecture intended to scare someone as they approached, like a Dominion SkyWatcher. People would remember this elegant ship, anywhere they went.

He had a lot of money stashed away in places nobody would find on this ship, if they needed to sell it and buy something new. Dave just couldn't see Vee parting with that last piece of his past.

He understood.

Hell, Dave had a book in his cabin that had been given to him by his father, decades ago. There were eight or ten people who would recognize it and know him immediately, regardless of disguise, but he wasn't ever getting rid of it.

Dave shook his head and considered all the ways they had gotten here, and where to go. A chime interrupted his reverie before he lost too much time. He had been up on the bridge of the ship, staring at the stars, as a break between watches and maintenance tasks that never ended.

Glaxu appeared at the back door when Dave called up a camera. He hoped it was Glaxu. He'd only ever met the one Mondi, so he had no idea how identical or distinct any given member of the species was.

"Hello?" Dave asked absently.

"Greetings, Tall Human," Glaxu said ritually, except it was more of a game they had fallen into. He did have a smile in his voice.

Glaxu called him *not-Dave-Hall* in private as a play on words, but could not do that on an open deck where there might be unwelcome ears. Even *Dave Hall* was dangerous to the wrong person.

"Good morning," Dave replied, keying the rear locks to unseat and allow the door to open. "Good nap?"

Valentinian took his personal security to a level of paranoia that even Dave marveled at, but it had kept them all alive, so who was he to argue?

"Most refreshing," Glaxu nodded to the camera as the door back there beeped politely. "Lunch is called for, but as you are on watch, I thought it would be helpful to keep you company as we ate."

Mondi did things as a nest, rather than individuals. Glaxu was the odd bird out, because he had adapted to the solitary lifestyle that had been thrust upon him by angry fates, but the bird had also accepted the rest of the crew as his new nest.

Dave checked his baton and pistol as he switched everything over to his card-reader and headed aft. Vee insisted on everyone being armed while on a station, regardless of being buttoned up. Something about burglars attacking the man previously.

Dave had his own enemies, so he would live the rest of his life expecting assassins to jump out from a closet. It was not a pleasant mental place to be, but not much had changed from his days as the Dominator, so he was at least used to it.

He met Glaxu aft, secured the rear hatch, and they

headed up to the kitchen. Mondi were predatory land birds, in the same way that humans had evolved from arboreal tree shrews, but Glaxu could process almost all of the food that Valentinian kept stocked. And the captain had wisely refused to install a herpetarium to provide Glaxu live snakes to eat.

Dave settled for a sandwich while Glaxu had dried, jerked beef that did a passable impression of snake.

"Not-Dave, I am concerned that we may need to confront your former mate," Glaxu said around bites. "Our Leader is the type who would avoid confrontation, until it is pressed upon him, at which time he would unleash a frightening level of violence. Can we frighten Athanasia off? Or do we plan to destroy her eventually?"

Yup. Warrior. Mondi nests were armed fighter squadrons, frequently acting as pirates, or would be if there was any recognized authority out here to challenge them. *Outermost*, Glaxu's ship, was heavily armed, but not armored enough to take on *Dominion-427* in direct combat. Probably, both ships would be destroyed in such a battle.

"Vee had talked about adding a turret for Kyriaki," Dave said as he continued to eat. "However, I think that we can only stay on this station for a few days before heading elsewhere on a longer circuit that eventually takes us back to Kryuome."

"Why is that, not-Dave?" Glaxu stabbed another bite with his beak.

"If she stayed around to look for us on the desert planet, that's about four days," Dave said. "We arrived here another day or two faster than she could, if she came direct. That should give us five days on station before we might find her off our bow blasting away and damning the consequences."

"So we shall flee?" Glaxu's voice had an edge to it he could not disguise.

Mondi didn't do evasion well. If they saw a problem, they attacked.

"What would Glaxu the Mondi, on foot, do against a Devincenzia?" Dave asked simply.

He had heard tales of the giant, flightless birds of Glaxu's homeworld. All beak and killing claws. Taller than Dave, and heavier.

Almost as mean.

"I would run madly from the beast until I could lure it into an ambush," Glaxu said, brightening suddenly like morning dawning. "Oh. Leader is baiting a trap?"

"To have found us at Kryuome, they had to have talked to one of only a handful of people on Bohrne Station, back in Laurentia," Dave nodded. "Once we left the desert planet, they could have perhaps guessed that we would end up here as Chatosig is the closest major industrial port. I have been studying the various planets in this sector of space, and this is the only significant system, from an industrial standpoint."

"And what will Athanasia do when she comes to this planet?" Glaxu asked.

"I don't know," Dave replied. "She should have quit before now, if she was going to, so she might never. If you weren't known as one of our associates, we could leave you here as a spy to watch, but that's too great a risk. We don't know if any of Truqtok's people survived long enough to talk to her about the dangerous, Mondi warrior who had killed so many humans."

They shared a grin. Vee and Kyriaki were dangerous in their own ways, but he and the Dire Ground Cuckoo had each killed many more than the others.

"Should I become a double agent?" Glaxu asked after another bite. "Remain behind and watch, but be prepared to share a story similar to Bayjy's, if approached by your humans?"

"That is a most dangerous game, my friend," Dave muttered carefully.

"And I am a most dangerous bird, Tall Human," Glaxu's eyes and headcrest grinned. "Perhaps Truqtok's minions could tell your ex-mate that, and you and yours decided I was too *something* to remain with you. Too alien. Too bloodthirsty. Ha, perhaps I just wasn't *dangerous enough* to remain in Leader's employ? You humans are *insane*."

Mondi's laughter sounded like a big cat chuffing in the grass. Dave joined him and flashed back to the ambush in the front quad of Truqtok's compound.

The one fool in the bed of their truck, aiming the twin pulsar at them, expecting them to be frozen with fear or to surrender. Except that Kyriaki had disabled it already, shot the man in the face, and Dave and his friends had unleashed a shitstorm of beam fire and detonators on the building.

Eventually, from a safe-enough distance, Kyriaki had managed to knock down the walls of the place with pulsar fire. And kill everything that had moved.

Yeah, maybe the Mondi was hell on stilts in close combat, and probably as a flier as well, but the rest of the team had internalized the need to take someone to the wall at the drop of a hat.

Slaughter everyone in the room and just assume that they needed killing.

Place like Truqtok's palace, you were likely to be more right than wrong. And the locals, the ones Dave would have called the aliens, except they were native and the humans were not, had approved of the outcome, once they were sure it had been contained.

A little touch and go there for a bit, but should be safe enough now. And the Widow had to deal with those folks after they had left. Or spend a lot of time at the south pole digging around, along with all the other losers.

"Perhaps, my wee, killer friend," Dave finally said as the laughter died down. "But the galaxy is an unsafe place, even after I spent twenty-five years trying to conquer it."

"Why were you unable to succeed, not-Dave-Hall?" Glaxu asked.

It hadn't been a topic of general conversation up until now. They had been busy trying to find buried treasure, and then to escape.

"It is extremely difficult to actually conquer an inhabited planet, Glaxu," Dave said. "I could drop tens of thousands of troops, but many of the places might have hundreds of millions of inhabitants. Better to just own the high orbital ground and install a favorable government. Fewer outright rebellions that way, and just a lot of friction to deal with. Still, I took eighteen, and successfully held on to nearly six hundred for my stretch."

Dave liked the way the headcrest popped all the way up and then poofed out sideways. He had learned that was the rough equivalent of a human's eyes bugging out and their jaw dropping to the floor.

Mondi were people. You just had to learn how to understand the non-verbal communications.

"That is an impressive feat, Big Guy," Glaxu finally choked out, using Bayjy's nickname for him. "And yet you retired to a life of an outlaw on the lam from justice?"

"Ended up there," Dave allowed. "I still have hope that we'll escape my wife at some point, and then things can settle down and we'll figure out what to do with the nest."

"So staying intact as a unit remains an option?"

"For the time being, it is the only option, Glaxu," Dave retorted. "Us against the galaxy. It might be years before alternatives become viable. My leaving does not protect the rest of you from retribution."

"No, it does not, most-lethal-human," Glaxu's eyes smiled. "Plus, I look forward to what this nest might accomplish, both in the realm of brigandry, as well as vengeance. Truqtok and his ilk will certainly not be missed. Perhaps something similar would be an effective use of your talents?"

"That would be Kyriaki," Dave said. "She had a law enforcement background. I'm just a killer."

"Indeed you are," Glaxu agreed. "But is that not what many situations call for?"

HE HAD BEGUN his fifth decade on this mad quest, accompanying the insane woman whose departure from the Dominion would salvage a bad situation and let the next regime take power without that many unnecessary executions to set the tone of things wrong.

Iulianus Palaiologos had understood from the beginning that his purpose was to keep her away from Cronus Prime forever, or at least until she fulfilled the one mission that would make them welcome her back, at least for a time.

Delivering Dave Hall's head on a platter.

The others would be a welcome addition, but none of them were valued highly enough to justify crossing the frontiers inward again.

Unless Iulianus was bringing the Widow's head, pickled in another jar as well.

Those had been his other orders, the ones delivered in secret by the Lord of the Dominion Armada itself: Keep her away, by hook or by crook, for as long as possible. Allow the old regime to fade without notice. Or end her, when that is no longer a viable option.

He had begun to wonder, from the way the woman acted, if she knew that. Or had perhaps guessed it. Much of her recent behavior made more sense that way.

Athanasia had become rage incarnate, distilled down to a fine cognac and bottled in crystalized malignancy. Iulianus wondered occasionally what the woman had been like before, when she still wore the half-mask that all elders of the Solar Party or Household maintained at all times. When things were measured with micrometers of social privilege and shades of cloth.

More than once, it had been his effort that allowed her to push the boundaries of the chase. Anything to get her farther away than yesterday. Eventually, they would enter a place where the Dominion itself was a legend, a tale told to recalcitrant children as a threat to behave. Be good, or the *Dominator* will come and get you.

They might be there now, heading through warp to a sector so distant that even his old Dominion charts, the finest available, had been marked with the equivalent of *Here there be dragons*.

Iulianus sat on his bridge and considered his next steps. It was night watch, and most of the crew was off-duty, doing the things that kept the ship in tune and the crew ready. Training, resting, studying.

He was alone up here, save for one helmsman, currently reading a novel on her main screen until the system needed human intervention; and a security trooper on the corner. Not one of the

Caelons, the Dominator's feared elite Assault Cavalry, and not one of Dominion Security's White Hats, although he had a team of those below, serving the Widow and guarding her.

It gave him time to think.

Iulianus's orders had carried him right up to the edge of what could have possibly been envisioned by his elders. Shortly, the Widow would reach a place where she would be able to separate herself from the rest of the mission, and in doing so would offer his crew the opportunity to mutiny in a most polite way.

Some would leap at the opportunity, he knew that. An Assault Courier such as *Dominion-427* was almost the worst possible dead-end assignment for an aggressive sailor in the Dominion Armada. All one did was haul around senior leaders in luxurious comfort, rather than participating in proper assault drops on hostile worlds and pirates. Some would seek the excitement missing from their lives, embracing the outlaw lifestyle as an escape.

For Iulianus, a proper officer would stay aboard his vessel, marking the mutineers off the rolls and returning to Cronus Prime, or even Dominion Prime itself, with the sad news of his failure.

However, his orders really did not allow that. Those orders that he could never discuss with anyone on this vessel, under any circumstances but the most extreme.

He would need to find a way to convince the Widow that he had undergone the same crisis of conscience, the same change of heart that would allow some of his crew to depart with the woman. Worse, the very act of doing so himself would cause too many others, the ones that would normally only waver, to fall into line behind him, convinced that it must be the *right thing to do,* if Captain Palaiologos was doing so.

A few sailors would turn to a flood. Except…

He wondered if it might indeed be a good thing.

What would he do when that moment arrived? If there were too many volunteers, *Dominion-427* might lack sufficient crew to return home with the few loyal ones.

His own preferences were not allowed to have any value here. The Widow would likely pass out of Dominion control at that moment and become a threat to the rest of the galaxy. That much was acceptable. But she might also decide to return home at some point and try to carve out her own place, which was not to be allowed.

Iulianus sat and watched stars streak by on the main screen. He would need to become perhaps the greatest double agent of all time. Allow himself to be seduced by the woman, to continue to remain close enough to her to kill her later if necessary?

He had seen the change in her eyes at the possibility that the mission might diverge now. The M'Rai, Vidy-Wooders, was a big, violent man. Probably the kind that could sate her with brutality, if that was the thing missing from her current needs. But he was also a junior varsity sailor, the kind who would have never even risen to the rank of an officer in the Dominion Armada.

The giant man had knowledge of Wildspace, but absolutely no business commanding a warship. Less, given his history with mistreating his previous crew.

Athanasia's next crew would have too many of Iulianus's current sailors for Iulianus to find that palatable. And she was not an unattractive woman, at least on the surface. Her core was an ugly, inhospitable place, but the relationship would only be physical, so far as he could manage it.

So he had begun the process of allowing her to see a person that she might find seducible enough to warrant the effort. Their relationship would not change much, as the Widow would still need to rely on a trained sailor to run things, even as she moved to the position of Owner, leaving him as commander.

Black widow or not, his orders, his core mission, allowed him no alternatives. Join the woman in her bed and her quest, regardless of the personal cost or the detriment of good conduct among his crew, especially as they began to be infected with piracy.

But keep her on the far side of Wildspace for as long as possible. Whatever methods, debaucheries, and lies were required. Whatever the personal cost to him and his crew.

At least until he had to kill her.

[11]

KYRIAKI

"You're selling him guns?" Kyriaki repeated, louder this time because he had apparently not heard her the first time.

Or Valentinian was ignoring her. She poked the back of his shoulder as she followed him through the armory.

The place was probably frightening to a civilian. Her fifty-member Internal Security Bureau detachment, back on Dominion Prime, might not have as many weapons available as Valentinian had stored in racks, floor to ceiling and everywhere else, in what had once been the ship's hydroponics greenhouse.

That green smell was long since gone, replaced with gun oil and ozone that had probably worked their way in the fabric of the walls by now.

Anuradhan technology had not been as efficient as the Dominion's was, at least in the realm of life support systems or weapons. Engines and overdrives were a whole other proposition. Upgrading *Longshot Hypothesis* to Dominion standard had allowed the previous owner to retire his hydroponics facility and turn it into some sort of storage.

Valentinian had put a lock on the door and filled it with every kind of firearm Kyriaki had ever even heard of, and many she had not.

"Some," Valentinian finally replied cryptically, stopping to look back over his shoulder while pulling a pulse carbine off the shelf. And a second.

That only left eight more on that rack. Plus the full rack below it.

"Any particular reason?" she asked, trying to force her way in past the shell he was carrying around today.

Something had happened since *Longshot* had docked at Chatosig-Six. She wasn't sure what, and the man was an exceptional card player, so he wasn't giving her any clues. But the conversation with Ozzo the shopkeeper had altered his trajectory somehow.

She saw a layer of pain in his eyes, when he finally met hers.

"Making changes," was all he said, brushing past her with the two rifles in hand and walking to a sled resting in the corridor.

For a man that didn't make changes unless forced, she wasn't sure that this was a good thing. Still, the prices Valentinian had been negotiating with Ozzo had been good ones.

Must be a market in mayhem and revolution around here.

Kyriaki came to parade rest: feet apart, shoulders back, hands crossed behind her; and waited for him to return.

He touched one of the five plasma rifles, shook his head, and continued deeper. She followed.

"Second law of thermodynamics," she quoted quietly as she ghosted up behind him. "There is no such thing as *good* news."

"Intimately familiar with that one, lady," Valentinian almost growled. "But there are necessary adaptations to circumstances, and mistakes. Hoping this falls more into the former."

"So what are you buying?" she asked bluntly.

"Connections and peace of mind, for now," he finally smiled at her. "Great big, freaking gun for you, later."

"Me?" she was almost jarred back a half step by the beaming smile on his face.

He had a pretty smile, when he wanted to use it. It reminded her that they had never actually kissed, as close as they had come over the last several months. Something or someone always intruded at the most embarrassing moment.

"Dave and I talked," Valentinian said quietly. "Can't take the ship off-line at a station or planet long enough to have all the work done that Bayjy suggested, but we can buy some tools and a lot of metal sheet and bar stock. Build out a new deck aft, over the cargo bay, and turn it into crew quarters and such, but we'll do it in deep space, just the five of us."

"And what about a gun for me?" Kyriaki asked.

"At some point later, we can install a telescoping ball turret on the top hull back there and put something big and lethal in it," his grin was back. "Lets you shoot back at people while Dave and I are flying."

"Oh."

She almost felt like someone had punched her in the stomach. Adding more space aft meant he could have a larger crew than the old days and still haul paying passengers around. But a gun turret meant that he was expecting her to still be part of that crew.

Like maybe they might really turn into a little more permanent than just the next few months. At least as a crew.

This close, his smell still did things to her mind that made her almost as angry as she was aroused. Kyriaki had never gotten her head fully wrapped around that, but neither had Valentinian. This was the moment when he might lean in and kiss her, if they had been in a romantic vid.

She might even allow it. But it would change things. And he didn't necessarily respond well to changes forced upon him by outsiders. Even her.

No, especially her.

They stared at each other for several seconds, across that impassible crevice that they had dug at some point. Or never filled in, which was almost the same thing.

He was thinking about it.

Kissing her.

She was thinking about it.

Valentinian glanced over her shoulder and started chuckling to himself.

"What?" she demanded in a sarcastic tone.

"This is where somebody walks in and catches us," he said between laughter. "Was expecting Dave to stick his head in and say something cute right about now. Need to have a talk with the screenwriters, or maybe the director, about their timing."

Kyriaki couldn't help herself. She joined him in laughing so hard that her stomach hurt and tears began to stream out of her eyes. Somehow, she found herself leaning against the man's shoulder.

Not in a romantic way, although each had gotten an arm around the other's waist, but just holding each other up as they laughed.

"Is this some human joke that would translate well into Mondi?" Glaxu interrupted as he stepped into the armory.

She and Valentinian doubled over now, alternately howling and gasping. Glaxu had a look on his face as if he wanted to mutter: *Humans…* with a really good eyeroll going, however politely he refrained at the moment that she looked.

Kyriaki reached up a hand and pulled Valentinian's face down. She didn't kiss him, but touched foreheads at the shared silliness of the entire thing. It was a human thing, and might not translate to Mondi, either.

Valentinian seemed to be reading her mind, because he started chuckling anew as their noses almost touched.

"You make me crazy," she murmured as she broke the contact and leaned back.

"Ditto," Valentinian agreed, taking a friendly step away from her, rather than the embarrassed one they normally fell into.

More chuckles. Maybe someone had released something into the life support system and she was stoned right now. Made as much sense as anything else.

"Glaxu," Valentinian finally asked as he got himself reasonably under control. "What are your preferences, for reach weapons?"

"Pistols light enough for my short arms and small hands," the Mondi warrior said. "I lack the upper body mass and strength of your kind. Monopod or crew-served light artillery is good for intermediate engagements, out to a range of…nine hundred human meters, if I do the conversion correctly in my head."

"Monopod?" Kyriaki leaned into the conversation. "What about a repulsor underneath?"

She found it cute the way his head rolled thirty degrees left, and the same again to the right, as if trying to see her from several angles, to understand her better.

"It would slow me down," Glaxu said with what she could only classify as an angry huff. "Find me a light rocket gun like not-Dave-Hall carries, lighter and in a smaller caliber, that I can carry over a shoulder, possibly in an undeployed state. Add a folding monopod and a sufficiently-capable lens atop, and he and I might have a competition at shooting down repulsor trucks and low-flying aircraft."

"Ammunition warhead matter?" Valentinian asked.

"Only in the special effects you would like to see at the far end of the battlefield. Sheathed copper over face-hardened steel would be sufficient at engagement ranges to probably poke holes in *Outermost*, which would be the measure of usefulness."

"The trucks don't have armor," Valentinian pointed out as Kyriaki listened.

"Humans have an endoskeleton around their brains and hearts," Glaxu said cheerfully. "Same as Mondi. Dead drivers crash even more effectively than dead trucks."

"Good to know," Valentinian said.

He gave her a smile as he turned back to the rest of the onslaught of firepower in here and handed her a slug-throwing chunk of wood and metal nearly as tall as she was.

"We'll add this to the sale pile," he said. "Ammunition is impossible to locate, a pain to make, and Dave's probably the only person here that could control the recoil."

"Then why do you own it, Captain Tarasicodissa?" Glaxu walked close enough to rejoin the conversation.

"The guy who owned it previously should have brought a pistol," she heard the laughter in Valentinian's voice. "Didn't want to leave it lying around, in case he woke up soon enough to take a pot shot at me before I got out of the camp and off the surface of the planet."

"I see," Glaxu didn't, but had picked up the human phrase from one of them. Probably Bayjy.

"Do they all have similar stories?" Kyriaki asked, gesturing around and relaxing finally from the emotional wringer of the last five minutes.

"Traded for about half of them," he offered with a shrug and an impish grin. "The stories go largely with what I traded them for originally."

"But we are in the market for more?" Glaxu's voice was hopeful with a fine, lethal edge to it.

"Absolutely. Need to protect my crew," Valentinian agreed, turning to look her right in the eyes, from almost close enough to kiss. "And my friends."

[12]
GLAXU

"Because most humans will be incapable of understanding Mondi body language well enough to catch me in a lie or prevarication, Captain," Glaxu answered with a slight head tilt, as if the human really should have figured out something so basic without help.

"She's not most humans, Glaxu," not-Dave-Hall answered from his place on the sofa.

Rather than have the conversation in the dining space, Captain Tarasicodissa had moved everyone into the lounge. Bayjy and Kyriaki were on the left, as Glaxu faced them, and the Tall Human was alone on the right.

He and Leader were pacing past each other as they argued politely.

It was nice to know such nervous habits transcended species.

"That is a thing of which I am highly cognizant, Dave," Glaxu said. "But I have had some experience misleading humans. Truqtok and his crew of cut-rate killers never attempted to overwhelm me because I had suggested that I was merely the leading edge of a larger, more dangerous force."

Glaxu paused to chuckle with the big man.

"At the time, I was not aware that I was not bluffing them," Glaxu continued. "But even the need for such misdirection presumes that they classify my species correctly, identify me as having been a member of your team, and then choose not to accept whatever wretched tale of woe I chose to spin."

"I'm not comfortable," Leader said, offsetting his stride so that they crossed in the middle of the room in separate lanes. "It puts you at too much risk, Glaxu. She's far more dangerous than those fools on Kryuome."

"Noted," Glaxu paused to study the man in command. "I offer it as a means of perhaps leading them astray. It would be easy enough to send them to someplace like Vorcia Thiri. Even an armed merchantman like *Dominion-427* would be at risk of attack, to say nothing of subterfuge. However, at present, we lack actionable intelligence of our foes. I propose to rectify that shortcoming in the cleanest method possible."

"*Dominion-427* is far more dangerous than an armed cargo transport," Dave pointed out.

"Not compared to some of the pirates and brigands that call Vorcia Thiri home, Dave," Glaxu replied. "Even my original nest ascertained that it was a wiser choice to depart the system with weapon systems armed, than to stay and press our luck. Perhaps the human variants and splinter kingdoms will choose to band together at some point and break the place, but for now it is something of an Urlan stronghold."

"Oh," Dave replied.

"Even Butler didn't go there," Bayjy opined. "And hardly nothing ever intimidated that fool. I like sending her there."

"Why has she continued to chase us?" Kyriaki spoke up, a mug of human tea, hot water strained through flavoring leaves, in one hand. "I feel like we haven't answered that question. It costs money to run any ship. And they aren't hauling cargo. She has to run out of cash eventually, unless she turns to piracy. Plus her crew can't be thrilled to be chasing us forever. Dave, how far would they go?"

"They should have stopped after Laurentia," Dave said. "Unless the Solar Party wanted her gone forever, which they might have. Dowager Widows don't really have a place in the power structure of the Household, since there is almost never a blood relationship to the new Dominator."

"Give her a ship and order it to follow her wishes?" Valentinian asked. "How long?"

Until they have achieved their goal, but Glaxu didn't say that out loud. He was *Farther*, and his ship was *Outermost*. Even his own kind didn't tend to see things with the same sort of obsessions that he occasionally brought to the nest.

Okay, more than occasionally. Habitually was probably a more accurate assessment.

Whatever.

"Until we're dead, or her crew mutinies," Valentinian said. "Let's just assume that we need to avoid the former long enough to create the latter."

"That's an interesting word," Bayjy pointed out.

"Mutiny. Your Dominion folks had to have planned for something like that. Does a mutiny mean they keep coming after us, even after ordered home by whoever was supposed to be in command?"

"I've spent too much time around the woman after Dave left," Kyriaki said. "She won't stop. Not until at least three of us are dead. Maybe all five, just to make sure there are no loose ends. What if 427's captain mutinies and dumps her on a station somewhere?"

"To give her that ship, and orders that got them to Kryuome, they don't want her back," Dave said. "Mutiny is maybe the wrong word, but I can't help but wonder if they might give her enough money, dangle it out there, that she could hire a replacement ship, staff it, and turn pirate while she continues hunting us. That lets 427 go home eventually, without her, but giving her enough rope that she'll keep going without them."

"All the more reason I should become a spy," Glaxu stopped his pacing in the middle of the room and faced them all. "*WE DO NOT KNOW*. And can thus not plan the correct ambush to eliminate her as a threat. Chatosig is an eminently excellent waypoint to make such a decision. She could buy a ship here, or be misled to head to Vorcia Thiri in pursuit of *Longshot Hypothesis*. Or perhaps her crew does mutiny, and leaves her here alone while they return home. At that point, she is a lame bilgebeast on an open plain and I might be able to eliminate her myself."

Glaxu fixed his gaze on Leader Valentinian. The man would ask the other three, and get their approval, but it was his decision, in the end. Sure enough, Captain Tarasicodissa looked at each of their cohorts and waited for them to nod before he proceeded. Each nest must have a leader, but that leader must maintain the support and respect of his followers.

Leader did that, and did it better than many of the nests Glaxu had known or served with in his time.

"Okay," Valentinian nodded to Glaxu. "We'll finish our trade with Ozzo and load up on metal stock and varied consumables over the next two days. Since nobody here knows us, we don't need a major argument on the deck to sell the story. *Longshot Hypothesis* will depart and aim in the direction of Vorcia Thiri, like we're looking for more trouble or a rougher place to hide. You'll have four sets of coordinates where we'll wait while we work. Questions?"

"Dave Hall, do you wish the threat neutralized, or eliminated?" Glaxu turned to Tall Human with his attention.

He had heard pieces of the tale, however far-fetched they were. Hopefully, Mondi weren't subject to the sorts of middle-aged depression that gave rise to something as immense and amazing as Dave Hall had done. Glaxu had never listened to his parents or elders well enough to determine if such things were fanciful allegories, or perhaps his future fears.

Dave Hall's face went through several emotional states in as many seconds. Glaxu did not know the species' communication morphologies well enough to follow the path, but eventually, Dave came to rest. Perhaps peace, but that was not quite the thing displayed.

"In the end, I expect that elimination is the only way that protects us," Dave replied darkly. "I had hoped she would give up and get on with her life, but I suppose it took me nearly two years to go through what she's probably facing now. If she appears at Chatosig, then she might never stop chasing us, so if you have a good chance to escape afterwards, killing her might be for the best for the widest number of people."

Glaxu quickly scanned the faces of the other humans, catching their emotional state.

He was still confused at the way that humans seemed frequently reluctant to simply open a foe's arteries with a quick dewclaw. Instead of nests, they had packs, and perhaps packsense was a stronger bond than Mondi maintained. They had to be brought hesitantly to the sort of calculated violence that secured their flanks.

Premeditated self-defense, one of Glaxu's instructors back home had called it. *Your Excellency, he needed killing.*

Glaxu nodded. This plan would protect his nest, and his friends. And quite possibly make the galaxy a safer place.

So damn it, when had he turned into one of the good guys?

[13]
ATHANASIA

Chatosig-Six.

Athanasia looked at the image, displayed on the bridge's main screen. There were a number of other stations in orbit, but the rest of them paled by comparison. Leaving off the industrial factories, this one station was larger than all the rest combined, running several kilometers of space across several decks.

Chatosig-Five, trailing in orbit, was where she would probably have to travel to actually take possession of a new ship if she commissioned one, but Six would be where she bought it.

Stephaneria sat with her to her left, enraptured with the view and possibly trying to spot the distinct hull of *Longshot Hypothesis* docked. Athanasia felt eyes watching her, the sense that the paranoia of the Dominion Household developed.

She turned and saw Captain Palaiologos studying her from under hooded brows. Shortly, the man's world would change, but she could not truly determine which way the captain would jump. Perhaps he didn't know, either, and she would have to bring him to the crux in order to force a decision out of him.

"We have arrived," he said in a definitive, if obvious tone.

They had.

Fate and destiny would intrude now. Or wash her out to sea like a riptide.

"Make your arrangements to dock, Captain," Athanasia replied. "Expect that we'll be here for at least a tenday, unless something unforeseen arises, so your crew should have time for station leave, as long as they are careful. Presume *Hard Bargain* is some distance behind us, and let him make his own docking arrangements, if he bothers to actually join us for the next stage."

She rose from her seat, off to the side of the bridge, and felt Stephaneria do the same. At times, the woman was almost an extension of Athanasia's will rather than her own being, but even from here, the need for revenge on Valentinian Tarasicodissa was almost a scent the younger woman gave off. Much like Athanasia's desire to end the one who called himself Dave Hall.

She would not use his true name. Dave Hall had given up the right to it when he had betrayed her and himself. He was just a fugitive now, a man with a significant bounty on his head and the enemy of all Dominion citizens. Laurentia would probably mint new currency with his face on it as a hero, but that was their decision.

She would settle for ending him.

"You will join me in my quarters when the ship

has safely docked, Captain," Athanasia fixed him with a cold eye, warning the man that decisions were now imminent.

Captain Palaiologos nodded exactly correctly in response to a woman of her station and she departed, Stephaneria a stride behind her and to the left as they made their way through corridors to her suite. Crewmembers they encountered hastened to step into side corridors or flatten themselves against walls as she passed, as if her very touch was toxic.

That it probably was toxic was beside the point.

Stephaneria came to rest at her side, once they were in the main salon.

"Should I fix you a drink now?" Stephaneria asked in a polite voice. "Docking should take perhaps an hour. There will be time to prepare for him."

"Yes, please," Athanasia nodded. "But remember that Iulianus Palaiologos must prepare for *me*. I have already laid the trap. He will either step into it, or around it, but that occurs now."

Stephaneria nodded silently and busied herself with bottles and glasses as Athanasia took a seat on the sofa and allowed a deep breath to calm her. It was almost as dangerous a situation as preparing annual budgets with the Solarians had always been. But she would prevail here, as she had there.

Her consort returned with two glasses and handed her one.

"Sit in the chair," Athanasia commanded lightly.

Otherwise, the woman might kneel at her feet and rest her head on Athanasia's knee. Such was the relationship they had settled into. Fire mixing with fire in the sleeping chamber, but much more controlled and shielded elsewhere.

Athanasia studied the lithe, former librarian who had transformed herself into the second harpy of the ancient trinity of vengeance. Idly, Athanasia wondered if she should recruit a third, just to complete the symbolic coven. Perhaps tomorrow.

"Our quest continues," Athanasia began, watching the impact of the words on the other woman.

"I faced decades of declining relevance and spinsterhood, my lady," Stephaneria replied softly. Not wistful. Perhaps a terrible rage carefully banked down like the blacksmith's forge fires. Athanasia wasn't sure how much of what she saw in the woman was rage, and what portion insanity. Stephaneria might not know. "The possibility of an occasional encounter with travelers, much as my uncle sometimes allows himself, but I am well past the age when a younger man would look upon me with naked lust. If vengeance on Tarasicodissa is to be the thing that sustains me, I look forward to bathing in his blood."

Yes, she may have been twisted beyond all recognition by those that might have once known her, but Athanasia knew how few friends the Librarian of Bohrne Station had accumulated. No other lovers since her divorce, leaving her emotions raw and easy to tap.

A fire that had been kept hidden.

Not for the first time, Athanasia wondered about the fool that had let a woman of such passion and intellect get away, but she supposed that those same things could intimidate a lesser man or woman.

Perhaps drive him to find a bubbly teenager with large breasts and not even such brains the Creator gave a sheep.

Men were like that. Unwilling to invest in the patience to unearth diamonds hidden in the stone. Intimidated by a woman smarter than they were. Or more capable.

And so the man had cast this amazing woman onto the ash heap of history for a floozy, without ever considering how much pleasure could be derived from those quiet passions.

"And after we sate our vengeance?" Athanasia asked.

She had to remind herself that there was a brilliant intellect there, however much the emotions had been warped over the short term. A woman smart enough to be appointed a Librarian. The Keepers of Knowledge, if not wisdom.

Stephaneria shrugged and took a sip of her drink. Athanasia did the same. Whiskey with a sweet/sour layer both above and below. Tart enough to keep you focused. Mellow enough to sand the edges off.

Yes, this woman understood the coming situation far better than she let on. Far better than anybody not in this room probably understood.

What else was she hiding?

"What will you do, with your purpose fulfilled?" Stephaneria asked. "You cannot imagine that the Dominion will welcome you back, even with Dave Hall's head on a spike."

"Indeed," Athanasia agreed. "They would fête me for a time, then retire me off to a quiet planet, far from the centers of power. Or perhaps arrange a quiet accident when nobody was watching."

"So you will remain in Wildspace," Stephaneria said. It was not a question, but an observation. And a keen one. "You will carve out your own power base here, presumably by building an empire or conquering one, and then live out your days as a queen. Perhaps you will be in need of a librarian. Perhaps not."

"And you have no strong feelings, one way or the other?" Athanasia asked carefully. Not surprised, but also not assuming anything, since everything was shortly in flux.

"I was hollow," the librarian said. "You found me, and filled me with purpose. Or fanned that anger that was already there when he left me for his floozies, but you gave me something greater to look forward to than brooding in anguish. I serve your body and your mission now, and in turn serve my own. I do not know what I will do. What place is there, for a middle-aged woman divorced and cast aside?"

"There is vengeance," Athanasia offered with a knowing smile.

She was also middle-aged and cast aside.

"Yes," Stephaneria agreed. "And I suppose that I might spend the rest of my life exacting it on the innocent men around me, or your Court if I chose that outcome. I could bathe in fresh blood regularly and teach them to fear all women, and not just the grand, evil Widow."

She laughed throatily, and Athanasia joined her. Had they time, she would have considered dragging the woman into the sleeping chamber to again tap that exquisite depth of emotional power. Were Stephaneria a man, Athanasia might find fulfillment in her alone, but there were still times she desired a different sort of pleasure instead. Perhaps as well.

But *Dominion-427* was waddling slowly into dock. Captain Palaiologos would join them shortly, and either be initiated into their conspiracy or cast from it bodily.

Athanasia hoped it was the former. He could serve her other needs far better than Butler Vidy-Wooders, she suspected. Most of them, anyway.

Taming a physical, intimidating monster like the M'Rai the hard way, breaking him to the bit, would be a grand adventure Athanasia looked forward to. And the first step to bridling all the other men she encountered.

She shared a devious smile with Stephaneria, wondering if the woman was sane enough to eventually become her successor.

Or just another victim.

[14]
IULIANUS

IULIANUS FACED the door with some level of trepidation. The woman within might not be a true praying mantis, but there was still risk. He must enter her lair now and convince this dangerous, dangerous woman of his sincerity in joining her cause.

If he failed, she would probably just send him home, where his mission would be a fiasco. If he betrayed her later, it would be an interesting question if he could sway enough of the crew to support him, or if his head would hang from the ship's bowsprit as a warning.

There would not likely be any middle ground available tomorrow.

Iulianus pressed the buzzer that would announce him. The door opened immediately, but those inside had felt the minor earthquakes that accompanied docking, so they had known he would be coming.

Inside the salon he walked, as far into her chamber, her life, as he had ever entered.

Again, that could change. It was possible she would demand physical submission, as well as emotional. It helped that the woman was still physically attractive. He could remain interested in her body.

The Widow stood in the middle of a space formed by two sofas and a chair. Cozy enough for conspiracies, which were only successful when they were kept small.

She had not changed clothes from the ankle-length belted tunic and leggings she had worn earlier, a dove gray cloth that hinted at impenetrable mists hiding cliff edges. The Widow's blond hair was up in a triple-braid today, with those in turn loosely tied together.

He had never seen her hair down, but it must come nearly to her knees unbound. Iulianus would only ever discover that after they were intimate.

If he survived.

The other woman was not present. The assistant they had brought aboard at Bohrne Station, so long ago emotionally. All the doors were closed, forming a compact conspiracy of two for now.

"Madam," Iulianus said as he came to the correct distance and bowed his head the precise amount her station demanded.

More would be too much right now. Less would be an insult best not delivered today.

"Captain," she replied in a cool voice. "Sit here, we must talk."

She gestured him to the near sofa, rather than the chair. It would allow her to sit close later, if she chose.

He risked it.

"Can I get you something to drink?" she asked in

a lighter voice, pretending that this was merely another social call.

"That would be preferred," Iulianus replied.

He would not drink so much as to impair his judgment, but a hint of alcohol right now would probably serve to lubricate the coming trial. At least she remained dressed like the warrior matriarch she was, rather than having changed into something perhaps intended to seduce his eyes.

Mind first. Body second. Soul never.

He watched her move with interest. Her face was too cold and precise, but when she turned away, she displayed the hard muscles in her back and bottom, those of a woman trained to the sword. That had not faded, regardless of the woman being nearly two decades older than he.

She glanced up from her bottles with a knowing smile on her face and in her eyes, as if she had displayed herself to him for exactly this reaction. Iulianus allowed himself to smile back, ever so fleetingly.

He could not imagine remaining in her employ, as mutineers or pirates, without some level of physicality. They were not children to shy away from such a thing. While he had never taken a wife, Iulianus had very little doubt who the woman's previous husband had been. No intelligent man would dare fornicate with such a woman.

At least, *before*.

Now, who was to say?

If his mission required abject stupidity on his part, at least her smile promised that he would enjoy it.

Two glasses mixed. Both tasted briefly as she

worked, confirming that the taste was correct. Hopefully, also that she had taken the correct antidote, if that was the agenda, and his death by poisoning would be quick and painless.

That might still be a preferable ending.

Iulianus smiled as she handed him a glass and returned to the chair, folding her feet under her gracefully, like a cat.

He sipped enough for the poison to presumably take hold. Whiskey with juice. Quite well done, too.

She smiled. He smiled. They drank and stewed in silence.

"How much latitude do your secret orders allow?" she asked abruptly, cutting through nearly thirty minutes of conversational gambits and evasions normally called for here.

Because he had spent the last tenday preparing for this conversation, Iulianus did not sputter denials or choke on the drink that he was taking as she spoke. That would also tell her things.

Perhaps she had already guessed at his purpose, or read his mind. Or was just that devious. But then, he already knew how dangerous this woman was.

"More than normal," he deflected the question, hopefully far enough to one side that he didn't end up bleeding afterwards.

"I can never officially return to the Dominion," Athanasia stated. "I think we can dispense with any charades to the contrary. If I remain here, I will need competent men and women, those I can trust, in key positions."

Iulianus nodded. She hadn't asked a second question. Hopefully, the other woman wasn't sneaking up on him right now with a garrote or something similar.

"Would you continue to serve me in some capacity?" Athanasia asked in a careful, sidelong way that seemed to track his mental evasions like a cobra watching the piper play.

Not *Will. Would*?

"I might," he offered. "Depending."

There. No more. No less. *What do you demand? What will you offer?*

"Empire," the Widow cast the words out into the hollow space between them, perhaps to see if the chasm would swallow them. "I have decades left in me, Captain Palaiologos. And wealth enough to walk off this deck and buy a ship of my own. From there, I intend to carve out my own place, rather than return to the Dominion as a beggar, hat in hand."

If she was who he expected her to be, without any confirmation, she was unlikely to wish to bear more children as possible successors to her crown, in addition to the two he knew of back in the Dominion. The Librarian would be young enough. Or there could be others.

"And my place in your vision?" he asked simply.

There was no edge to the tone that might insult or anger the woman. Merely a man asking to clarify something he did not clearly understand the first time.

"I need someone like Butler Vidy-Wooders for his knowledge of Wildspace," she said. "At least until I find someone better. Almost anyone will do at this point. I will never trust that man to command a ship I own. Bohrne Station clarified for me what kind of creature that M'Rai truly is. I need someone I trust to command a warship in my service. To command fleets, when I build them."

She paused there, dangling the bait in front of him, probably just to see if his price was that low. Or if his secret orders left him that little latitude.

Iulianus shrugged slowly and deliberately. He watched her with flat eyes. The kind she probably saw in the mirror when she forgot to pretend she was someone else.

"I will have other needs, as well."

Her voice had taken on a smoky tone now. A woman speaking, and not just an inviolate queen carved from the blue depths of an iceberg.

Iulianus allowed himself to study the woman as a woman now. Ogle her some, as she watched. If she was offering herself, he would need to understand what that quagmire promised. As much as he might enjoy her.

"I could simply depart with *Dominion-427*," he smiled in a rough, biting sort of way. "Anything less would technically be mutiny on my part, depending on how they would interpret my various orders."

Plural. Public and secret. Who knows what they told me to do?

"And what would you return to, Captain?" her own edges came out now. "Another decade or three of flying important busybodies around Dominion Space? Perhaps a desk job at some sector base where you count the days until you retire, and then the days until you die?"

"It is a safer bet than dereliction of duty becoming piracy, madam," he countered carefully.

"And a more boring one, as well, Captain," she

smiled. "Out here, there is the potential for danger, for wealth, for glory. If you wish to take it."

"Is that all?" he drawled, allowing his eyes to show off the least amount of leer.

If you intend to seduce me into sedition, Widow, the price you pay will be so much higher than mere piracy. Nothing you can't meet, but nothing you can wave off cheaply either.

Perhaps your soul.

Her smile suggested that the tendency of the conversation did not surprise her. Nor, possibly dismay her either.

"There are other rewards one might aspire to, Captain Palaiologos," her voice drifted lower and became almost sultry as he listened. "But those require a deeper commitment."

Yes, he had no doubts about that. Praying mantis. At least if he stepped wrong.

But at a deeper level, she was right. What *did* he have to look forward to? He would never command one of the great warships in battle. Never stand in high orbit over some prostrate planet as his assault squadrons fell from the sky. He would perhaps be rewarded by the Lords of the Armada for returning her head in a vacbag. Doubly so if he also had Dave Hall and the others with him at the time.

What would it gain him? As she had said, perhaps a notation in a file that the man was more dangerous than originally calculated. Or perhaps not. They had chosen him for this mission. Certainly a medal of some sort, then. Promotion to the ground somewhere, where folks might remark how important he was, as he slowly atrophied into senescence.

Retirement then. Death at some point after that. Nothing that would mark his passing.

Iulianus Palaiologos could not remember the passions of his youth that had driven him to Dominion service. He had lived a careful, deliberate life and career for more than two decades. It had brought him here.

Wherever here was.

He recognized the precipice. Wondered if the Lord of the Dominion Armada would be surprised by his choices, or if they already knew his vision of duty would drive him to apostasy.

The Widow was offering herself as the ultimate reward for his loyalty. If they survived piracy, presumably there would be other things that might sate his fancy.

He would have to think up things to fill in that empty place in his soul that duty and service to the Dominion had once fulfilled. As she said, she could not return, any more than he could if he accepted.

"I will need to think," Iulianus offered as an evasion, a delaying tactic.

As if he hadn't already gamed this scenario out many times, with outcomes that ranged from him dead on the deck of poison to a rambunctious threesome in the main sleeping quarters with the librarian from Laurentia.

"You do not have long, Captain," she purred at him, smiling as if she had already won. "My mission will not wait."

"Please, call me Iulianus," he said, moving them beyond the mere relationship of politician and servant to something darker. Deeper.

More dangerous.

"In private," she said with a gleeful smile, as if she had already burned her brand into his shoulder. "And you will call me Athanasia, Iulianus."

"Athanasia," he said, tasting the power of her name and wondering where it would take them next.

But everything else was a performance now. He would allow himself to be seduced from his formal duty by dreams of lust and avarice.

He might even live to enjoy them.

$$[\ 15\ ]$$

GLAXU

Longshot Hypothesis was successfully away, and Glaxu was playing at being bereft and lonesome. *Outermost* had been moved to a cheap dock, the sort of long-term place where locals might store a vessel. It was a long walk from anyplace interesting, in one of the older, more worn sections of the station.

Exactly the place for a sailor down on his luck. At least as far as the humans and their cousins would interpret things, according to Leader, Big Guy, and the two, dangerous women: Bayjy and Kyriaki.

Glaxu settled on a bar stool designed for a fat human. The seat was round, forty centimeters across and the thing was tall as he was. But it was a perfect height for him to squat and see over the bar.

He wore his long shorts today, the heavier ones that he needed when the heat was so low that his ankles would start to hurt. The longer squatting cloth as well, since he could fold that over his legs like a blanket and remain warm as he sat still enough for heat to bleed off.

Glaxu had even gone so far as to dig out a sleeveless shirt and wear it under his crossed bandoliers and belt, covering up his chest feathers.

Humans had an entirely different perception of hot and cold than Mondi did. At least Bayjy understood where the thermostat should be set. If he stayed in human space for too long, Glaxu expected that he would have to invest in gloves and earmuffs.

And pray nobody ever managed to take a picture of him.

However, the bar's interior was wood, hauled up to orbit at great expense, even as a veneer, so his general fabric shades of taupe did not stand out, except contrasting with the aged copper surface of the bar where his drink rested, slowly steaming.

Apparently, the humans even drank their fruit juice refrigerated, which was all sorts of wrong, but the bartender had enough experience to not argue about steaming it to the proper temperature for a Mondi.

Glaxu presumed that the next one of his kind that ever graced such an establishment would thank him, if the knowledge of how to serve good drinks stuck.

He had chosen this restaurant because the officers of *Dominion-427* were lazy. It was the closest place to where their own ship was docked, and they had immediately gravitated towards it with the sorts of mindless placidity he normally expected from herd animals.

Prey.

But that was a rude way to conceive them. The humans as a species were probably the most treacherous in space these days. Others were more violent, individually, but humans were pack hunters, like Mondi, and you never faced just one. Leader had taught him just how dangerous a team of humans could be when agitated to violence.

The group approaching today wasn't a team. Four of them appeared to be officers of the Dominion Armada, based on the clothing descriptions not-Dave-Hall had supplied, including the commander of the vessel. A fifth was a female human in civilian garb.

The sixth was the one to watch. Athanasia. The Widow of not-Dave-Hall. Of a height closer to Bayjy than Kyriaki. Of a build and coloration more like the smaller woman. Of a temperament, as well, dark and cold. Lethal but quiet.

Glaxu had a spot at the bar where the corner wrapped the square. It made him almost a pocket nest, but there was one more chair beyond him, deeper into the corner if one wanted to sit so close to an obvious alien. An obviously-armed alien. In a space that had less than one third of its capacity currently filled.

Their dinner was a formal, brittle affair as he watched, judging from what little he had learned of human body language from Truqtok's people, and Valentinian's. The rest were carefully deferential to Athanasia, as they had been previously.

It helped that Dave had been able to tell Glaxu the exact clock schedule the crew of *Dominion-427* probably still kept, based on the time patterns of a place called Dominion Prime, several sectors away.

Stations were constant things, but even they tended towards light and dark cycles based on the planet they orbited. *Dominion-427* was well off that schedule, and still as predictable as death and tax levies.

He had watched variations of the group previously from his perch at the side of the bar. Not obvious, but he was the least like the standard patterns of erect, simian, bipeds in the room, so Glaxu knew he stood out.

But he had a good cover identity established. Ozzo the shopkeeper could place him in context with *Longshot Hypothesis*, when enough people began to ask around.

Valentinian had once said that all fixers appeared to be cousins, across species and systems. Glaxu had no reason to doubt that logic. Mondi hunters were no different.

Eyes studied him now. Two more heads were turned his direction from the six at the table, leaving only one not at least glancing his way.

In any other situation, Glaxu would have drawn a weapon and held it close to the invisible side, away from the humans, so he did here as well. He was already wearing his shock bracers, however uncomfortable they were to sit on for long periods, because he had promised Valentinian that he would not accidentally dewclaw somebody's life out all over the deck in a wet, messy mistake.

Mistake being the operative phrase. He could still easily knock some fool down, stun them silly, and then take off a bracer. If somebody really pissed him off. Even humans seemed not to be so dim as to miss that option.

Words were murmured over there. Glaxu regretted not having his helmet with the advanced electronics on. Then he could have listened in on their conversation, as well as measured their skin temperature, heart rate, and the pupil dilations of the ones looking this way.

Just to stay in character, he flipped the safety off. Even six humans weren't a threat in a room like this. He could use the bar, the stools, the tables, and even the other humans as obstacles and weapons. They'd be better off hosing this area of the room down with plasma rifles, but none of them were armed with anything more than polite pulse pistols. Dangerous in the right hands.

Maybe two of them qualified over there, not counting the younger, civilian female who didn't move like a sailor, a dancer, or an assassin. Her purpose with the group was not clear.

The command officer rose, eyes carefully looking this direction, but face utterly neutral. At least he was smart enough to keep his hands in clear sight and open at his sides as the man moved this direction.

Glaxu shifted around so that the bar was at his side, the one with the pistol. The man noted the stance and adjusted his path to remain on the outside, rather than crossing behind Glaxu to box himself into the corner.

Glaxu doubted that the human understood head crests, but he kept things compact for now, rather than up and spreading in a threat display. He let his eyes talk instead.

"Captain Redtip Windrunner?" the human asked in a quiet voice as he came to rest just behind the empty stool around the corner.

Glaxu nodded in a friendly, offhand manner. Like one of the tree shrews could mistake the only Mondi on the station.

"I am Captain Palaiologos," the human said. "Commander of the vessel *Dominion-427*. I was hoping you might be available and interested in talking."

So, some fixer cousin had already reached out to these people and filled their oversized ears with idle chatter and silly lies. In just two days. The tales Valentinian had planted before he left.

As Leader had expected.

"About?" Glaxu asked in a clipped tone he understood sounded bored to human ears. A Mondi might try to whap his headcrest for it, instead.

"It is my understanding that you recently worked with a ship known as *Longshot Hypothesis*," the man explained himself without any physical motion that might get him shot. His crew likewise remained still enough to not provoke. "And that the ship left for a different system while you remained."

Glaxu eyed the oversized, tree shrew. Any smart operator would smell a trap. And it was.

But what kind of trap was it? Whose?

"They are merchants, human," Glaxu tutted rudely. "Not warriors. The captain was too worried about shipping margins for me to ever fit in with his kind."

Which was only partially a truth. Valentinian had done an admirable job of translating moneymaking endeavors from piracy or security work into what humans did to explore and expand into other folks' space. *Outermost* would never carry significant cargo, but Glaxu made an excellent caravan guard.

If he could ever find anyone dumb enough that they deserved to be shoot.

"Do you know where they went next?" the man asked in an offhand way.

Oh, you think I'm stupid enough, or perhaps angry enough, to just give you information? No, I think you'll have to purchase it at retail rates, tree shrew.

"Why?"

"My superior would be the one to explain that," he said.

Glaxu looked past the human and studied the tall blond. The true power here.

Humans might make the mistake of thinking that a Mondi not focused on them would miss movement. Snakes frequently made a similar mistake. The captain didn't take the bait. Neither did the other humans.

Pity. Dave and Kyriaki had both explained how to make something look like self-defense, at least in the aftermath. It certainly would have solved most of Valentinian's problems, for Glaxu to kill the commanders of the fools chasing him across the galaxy. But he couldn't count on surviving afterwards, even in a nicer place like this.

"What's in it for me?" Glaxu drawled in a tone that would have caused a duel back home.

"Again, she would be the best one to negotiate such a matter," Captain Palaiologos replied neutrally. "I am just the messenger here."

Yes, you would be, wouldn't you?

Glaxu nodded to the human in the accepted, interspecies manner and watched the man back carefully away. He had already paid, but Glaxu left another coin on the bar for the tender as a thank you for getting the juice just right.

And to perhaps mark the Mondi as a good customer, in case all hell broke loose in the next five minutes and Glaxu ended up splattering human blood all over the tables, floor, and other patrons.

Five of these people looked like bilgebeasts ready for a spring shearing. Only the blond woman carried herself like a warrior.

But then, Dave had been mated to the creature for a long period, so she probably had to be capable of violence.

Hopefully, not as good as a Mondi.

[16]

ATHANASIA

Until she had left Dominion space, Athanasia wasn't sure she had ever met a truly alien species. Most of the Dominion was comprised of pure human, not even interspersed with the so-called Variant Humanities of Wildspace and very few humans even darker than the pinkish-white tones she was most familiar with. Laurentia had a few near-humans running around, the kind that you might not realize weren't, if you encountered them naked in the dark.

This creature was alien.

Ground bird, with long legs, short arms, long beak, and big eyes. Clearly intelligent and tool-using, just from the clothing and equipment it wore. Barely a meter tall, most of that legs and neck. Perhaps eighteen kilograms soaking wet.

It moved like a killer. Athanasia had known enough of those in her time to tell the difference between baneful and lethal. She watched him holster

97

a pistol he had been holding to his side as Iulianus had approached.

Eyes quick-scanned the others, lingered briefly on Stephaneria, and then ignored the sailors entirely. Not a bad risk analysis.

A chair had been pulled close to the oval-shaped table. The creature caught a foot on the crossbar and popped right up onto the seat, squatting quickly down in such a way that only made him look smaller than her.

Athanasia wasn't fooled one bit.

"Who are you?" the birdman demanded of her in a bold, bald opening.

"An Ambassador from the Dominion," Athanasia replied with enough of a partial truth.

That was the rank she had been assigned, as a means of putting the ship under her authority.

"And I am the only being in this room that's ever even heard of such a place," he sneered. "Unless you accidentally run into a cartographer who's lost."

Athanasia caught the joke in the creature's words, but suspected that it went right by everyone except Stephaneria. Possibly Iulianus noted it, but he had retreated into his formal shell in public. The man he had been for the last several months, perhaps years, rather than the one who might turn into a co-conspirator in the near future.

"We're hunting Valentinian Tarasicodissa," Athanasia offered.

"You're the reason he tucked tail and fluttered at Kryuome?" the birdman whistled in a way she could only classify as derisive.

So, she had the right creature. The bribes she had

spread around had led her to the one that survivors at Meeredge whispered about.

The few survivors.

"Probably," she said. "The man is a wanted criminal with a bounty on his head."

"How much?"

Athanasia quoted a figure that the authorities back home would gladly pay, because the only way someone was taking Tarasicodissa's head in also involved including Apokapes and Dave Hall in the deal.

Again, a whistle. More interested this time, perhaps.

"Who'd he kill for that kind of reward?" the birdman known as Redtip asked.

"One of his crew is an assassin," Athanasia offered.

"The tall one or the blond?" the creature replied, confirming that he had known the crew of *Longshot Hypothesis* well enough to judge.

"The male," she said.

"Interesting," the creature nodded. "I still suspect the blond is more trouble, but they didn't kill enough people for me to really judge their relative abilities there. So?"

"So," Athanasia countered.

It was hard, doing this with a true alien. The body language was completely different from anything she had ever encountered, and Athanasia couldn't rely on femininity as a secondary weapon.

She wasn't even sure if the creature was of a bi-gendered species, and it would be rude to ask right now.

"So I would like to see what your price might be for information, or perhaps assistance," Athanasia ventured carefully.

The creature cocked his head left and then right, as if a predator studying his lunch before striking. Glanced once around the table again, lingering briefly on Stephaneria before returning to her.

"Why should I care what the featherless do to one another?" it asked her in a tone that seemed calculated to range exactly midway between sarcasm and insult.

"You probably should not," she said. "If you are no longer associated with them, I presume you'll get on with your life and eventually I will continue after them, once we determine where the ship has gone."

"Eventually?" the creature caught the key word. Apparently it was better at speaking Spacer than most aliens, and many humans.

"I have business at Chatosig first," Athanasia said.

"Need someone killed?" the birdman popped up and eyed her in a way she could only classify as *hungry*.

"Later," Athanasia offered as a morsel, just to see if the thing would strike. "First, I have shopping to attend."

The head retracted again, almost deflating back to the compact form it had first assumed.

"When you need killing done, you let me know and I'll make you a great deal," it said suddenly, hopping quickly off the chair and backing away with a bobbing head. "'Til then, I'll be around."

And with that, it sauntered away, not once

looking back as it cleared the front hatch and disappeared around a corner.

"That was…interesting," Stephaneria said in a calm, detached voice.

Athanasia smiled lightly. Not what she had been expecting, but then, she had assumed the little creature was a spy, left behind by Tarasicodissa to deflect them onto a different course.

She wondered if the concept that *Dominion-427* not going anywhere immediately was enough for the bird to flee to his master, or if she had gauged the situation wrong and the little monster was too much a warrior to have any interest in anything except violence.

That would also explain why it had parted ways with the others. They were in an unarmed freighter, looking for trade opportunities and trying to keep a low profile, even as they were being chased across the galaxy.

"Interesting, yes," Athanasia agreed. "Now we get on with our other plans."

Iulianus had a look in his eye like he wanted to say something, but had hidden himself back behind those walls so carefully that he might not be able to escape again for a while.

"Captain?" Athanasia asked.

"We asked no questions, volunteered little information, and he flounced off as if bored," the man observed critically. "Were we wrong in our estimations?"

"Oh, no, Captain," she smiled. "That was merely the opening moves of what will become an incredibly complex game. We will remain on our usual schedule, to allay spies, and see if the little beast is still here tomorrow."

"And if he is?" Stephaneria asked.

"Then we convince him to lead us to Valentinian."

[17]
GLAXU

GLAXU WISHED that his face was capable of the kind of broad grin that humans adopted when things went well. Fools had assumed him to be a dumb wing-gun, rather than a flank hunter, and not once guessed that he had used the opportunity of stepping up onto the chair at their table to stick a small listening device onto it.

Everything they said was being recorded right now, by a tiny device just waiting for him to send a signal so it could dump its brains in a complex burst.

He jogged hard, once he was out of immediate sight of the dock where the Dominion vessel and a few guards were stationed. Humans would probably drop their lower beaks in shock, watching him move, but he wasn't even running that fast. Only about half again quicker than the best human could do on his best day.

It got him to his ship while the group was still seated and eating dinner, so he skipped the recorded bits and listened in real time to their conversation.

Flank hunter, blond lady. The one that sweeps long and herds fools into the nest's guns, or suckers them into chasing.

Outermost.

Farther.

Dave had warned him that Dominion folks tended to be specist shits that assumed intelligence declined as one moved away from the upright, hairless tree shrew morphology. Glaxu hadn't seen it with *Longshot's* crew, but the last couple of days on the station had shown him just how different Leader and the others were from the rest of their kind.

Wildspace didn't allow that sort of intellectual superiority complex to remain for long. He might be unique on this station as a Mondi, but there were a number of Urlan around, as well as Sh'Vaadig, Viddhu, and Daicia, just along the stretch as he had made his way back to his ship. The Gazetteer had listed forty-plus species in residence at Chatosig-Six, splitting all the Variant Humanities into their own flavors based on ability to interbreed.

This Athanasia woman was sharp, he had to give her that. But arrogantly specist in the worst ways, assuming he was too stupid to work a seven-layer betrayal into his plans. She was expecting to triple-cross him.

Seriously, a Mondi?

Glaxu was almost insulted enough to just ambush them with guns at some point and splatter the decks with their blood. He would have to do something like that indoors, because Station Security would take an impatiently-dim view of him flying up to their Dominion ship and hammering it with cannon fire from *Outermost.*

Chatosig-Six might be a civilian station, but that didn't mean that they didn't command a broad swathe of orbit with their heavy cannons. As much fun as it might be to try, Glaxu doubted that even he could successfully evade ground fire long enough to make it to the buoys and escape. Plus, Valentinian wanted to return to this system and this station at a later date, and wouldn't appreciate having to make allowances for a stubborn Mondi who had to park his ride elsewhere and catch a boost.

Still, he would have grinned, had his beak allowed it.

[18]
VALENTINIAN

"I'M JUST CONCERNED," Valentinian griped, looking around the room at the smiling faces as everybody ate dinner.

"You don't think he can handle it?" Dave asked, taking a sip of stew.

"Oh, I think he can," Valentinian answered. "I just have a hard time trusting a relative stranger with all our lives, even if he has been pretty good up until now."

"You think Glaxu would sell us out?" Kyriaki's eyes bored in on him.

"I'm pretty sure they're going to offer a tremendous amount of cash to him," he said. "Or worse, they figure out he's a spy and threaten to kill him, and he has to roll over on us to buy his life, if he can. Either way, we'd be deep in trouble with not a lot of time to react."

"He's done nothing to justify burning him, Vee," Dave said carefully.

"Which is why I haven't changed our schedule, or

moved the ship," Valentinian said. "You asked why I was so nervous and I answered you."

"True," the Big Guy shrugged. "Are you that worried?"

"Everything worries me, Dave," Valentinian laughed harshly. "Welcome to the life of a tramp ship captain. Every single thing I do has to be geared towards keeping the ship and the crew running at best efficiency with the amount of funds and time I have available."

"He'll be fine," Bayjy jumped into the conversation. "Deadly, little bird had Truqtok's people afraid of him before we came along. *He* might have been junior varsity, but the Widow can't be that deadly, can she?"

That last was spoken in Dave's direction. All the heads came around and the Big Guy stopped eating long enough to look around.

"The woman I abandoned on Cronus Prime would have chased me at least this far, I think," Dave said succinctly. "Since Glaxu hasn't shown up in the first window, we can presume that she made it as far as Chatosig in the expected time. Had we just flown the long ways across Wildspace from there, we probably would have lost her, and then the only time she ever showed up again in our lives becomes a black swan event so improbable as to be incalculable. But she's got to be running out of rope, at least as far as the Dominion is concerned. I would have thought her crew would refuse orders after Kryuome, but Glaxu's not here, so presumably she's there and he's dancing with her."

"What orders would her crew have gotten?"

Valentinian asked with his head turning sideways. He had an idea that really didn't make him happy.

Dave had gone pale and still, like the big guy hadn't really given it a lot of thought until now. Valentinian had.

"Keep her out of Dominion space," Dave said slowly. "Probably however they thought they could reasonably do it, without killing the woman."

"Assault Courier is an expensive ship to maintain, right?" Kyriaki leaned towards him.

Valentinian noted how much drawl had entered her tones now, as well.

"Yes," Dave nodded. "DropShips are raw metal inside, but Couriers are for important people, so lots of extra fittings and such."

"She's smart enough to see the end of the rope coming quickly?" Bayjy asked.

Valentinian leaned back a little, just because maybe the other three were coming to the same spot he was already at in his calculations.

"She is," Dave nodded slowly.

Everything was in slow motion now.

"Chatosig was closest to Kryuome for an industrial hub," Bayjy said. "That's why I picked it for us. Just also happens to be shipyard heaven, for reasons we don't talk about in polite company."

"Piracy," Dave agreed.

"Pirates need ships," Kyriaki spoke up.

To Valentinian, it was like the two women were completing each other's thoughts aloud, in a bizarre harmony that brought home to him how much those two had turned into friends instead of coworkers or rivals.

Dave nodded. So did Valentinian. So did Bayjy.

"Good place to buy a ship with a lot of guns and armor," Bayjy took up the thread. "If you have funds handy, and maybe a crew getting restive to go home."

"Not everyone is going to be as persistent as the White Hats, or the Widow," Kyriaki spoke in turn.

"So we suspect that Athanasia is going to Chatosig to buy herself a replacement for *Dominion-427*?" Dave asked. "Recruit as much of the old crew as she can turn into pirates, and keep coming after us in a new vessel none of us know?"

"Glaxu probably knows," Bayjy said serenely. "Or will, soon. Y'all don't give that boy credit for subtlety and guile like you should."

"Okay, Vee, I really do owe you an apology," Dave nodded deeply. "It's just crazy enough of an idea that I could see her doing it. And we'd be in a bad spot, if some random ship could just sail up to us and open fire. Do we need to sell the *Longshot Hypothesis* in the near future and find something else to hide in so they don't know it's us?"

"That's not my preference, Big Guy," Valentinian said. "But we might not have a choice."

"Do we stop the work aft on the new deck?" Bayjy asked.

They had been here eight days now. If Glaxu had decided the Widow wasn't coming, he might have arrived as early as yesterday.

Valentinian considered it.

They had made a hell of a run at the job, turning the gravity off for four hours at a time so they could move big plates and structural beams around and then tack weld them into place. None of it would stand up to hard maneuvering or incoming beam damage, but they would have the frames good enough by tomorrow that they could move on to plumbing, wiring, and rooms.

"No," he decided. "In for a gersh, in for a drachma. But I'm going to program the overdrive with an escape course I can trigger from back here, if we get pinged by anybody while we're working in zero gee and can't get to the bridge quickly."

"Is that paranoid enough?" Kyriaki asked.

"Which takes me right back to where Dave started this," he grinned at her. "Do we trust Glaxu's competence and loyalty enough to not move the ship from where we are right now? Do we hightail it clear across Wildspace as the only way we can escape the Widow, and not come back to look at Kryuome for at least a year?"

"I got a good feeling about the Mondi," Dave offered. "And I've had to judge a lot of people accurately over the decades, frequently on the flimsiest of evidence, when I was the most feared warlord in space. But yeah, let's move some black swan plans up in our priority list. Shame we didn't go ahead and buy that surplus gun turret Ozzo's friend had for sale."

"It might still be there when we get back," Kyriaki said. "If not, we'll find something else. It wasn't that great a deal, with the amount of work I would have had to do before I was comfortable firing it. Old and neglected, off a paranoid captain who installed it, and then maybe never fired it again for years, even to test it. We can do better."

"Understood," Valentinian agreed with everyone. "After lunch, I'm going to abandon you for a while and spend some serious thinking time up on the bridge while you weld stuff aft. Goal right now is sturdy enough to handle maneuvers. We'll make it pretty later."

"I don't know about y'all, but my shit's already pretty, thank you very much," Bayjy huffed at them.

Valentinian joined the others laughing. It felt good to release some of the tension that had kept him up at night.

Things were completely out of his hands now, and would be until something happened. Then he might be too busy running for his life.

Again.

AT LEAST THE creature had bathed. Iulianus was looking for small victories here, and the fact that the always-tardy M'Rai Captain, Butler Vidy-Wooders, had actually stepped into a shower with soap, and combed the mass of unruly hair and beard into something vaguely approximating orderly, probably qualified, based on the things Iulianus had heard about the man prior.

And seen himself.

Apparently, the Urlan Empire, at its height, had engineered any number of human sub-species into specific worker contingents. Captain Tarasicodissa of *Longshot Hypothesis* supposedly had a Pranai crewmember, designed with little body hair, higher muscle content than normal, and preference for extreme heat. Other designs did other things, based on the monstrous egos of the scientists, intend on maintaining slave species rather than developing technological automation.

The M'Rai had been built as foremen and

brutalitarians. Three meters tall, or just a shade under, so that Iulianus was staring at the center of the thing's chest when both were standing. Massively muscled and bulky, capable of lifting feats normal humans could not achieve. And violent.

The intellect appeared to be a bit lacking, but if Iulianus had been going to build brutes to keep the other slaves in check, he wouldn't have made them all that smart, either. No reason to tempt a slave revolt.

From what Iulianus had been able to ascertain, Vidy-Wooders was rather median for his species. Size and a bully complex had put him in a position to buy a ship, hire a crew, and then luck had let him make a huge discovery worth a tremendous amount of money.

Then the M'Rai, in his stupid shortsightedness, had dumped his crew on a station back in Laurentia, rather than paying them their share, apparently unable to grasp the reputation he would build for himself overnight.

They don't call you Butler the Bridge-builder, do they?

But that was probably a crudity uncalled for in this situation. The man was more or less hat-in-hand today, if Iulianus was interpreting the signals correctly. Bathed and cleaned. Fresh clothes lacking any food stains, at least so far.

Even his attitude had improved from the semi-drunken aggression previously seen.

Still, Butler the Bridge-builder.

"Welcome, Captain," Athanasia rose from her seat in the ship's main salon as the man was escorted into the room. She gestured for Vidy-Wooders to sit on a chair specifically purchased on the station for the man's size and bulk.

Hopefully, he would see that as a positive sign on the Widow's part, and not get any more objectionable than normal.

The M'Rai moved carefully, aware that the ceiling above his head didn't have much clearance in here, as the ship had been built for standard-model humans.

The woman Stephaneria, the Librarian with the violent eyes, served the man a drink that was a rum punch heavy on the juice and rather light on the alcohol. Enough to put the man at ease, hopefully, but not push him into an out-of-control place.

Iulianus noted the two White Hats carefully waiting in the inner corners of the salon, where they would be behind the giant if he got out of hand and needed to be put down. Athanasia was also not taking any chances today either, as much as she was trying to be accommodating.

"Sorry I'm late," the M'Rai mumbled as he tested his great weight on the chair carefully.

As he was on time today, Iulianus assumed the man was referring to being behind schedule in warp, first to Kryuome, and now to Chatosig.

Apparently, firing your mechanics meant you had to do all their work on the ship yourself instead. Who could have imagined that?

"You are here, now, Captain," Athanasia exuded a grace and charm wasted on the beast in the big chair, but Iulianus understood the need.

They lacked the intimate knowledge of Wildspace that only a native could bring to the table, and there were few that the Widow could so easily put a leash on as Butler Vidy-Wooders.

As an example of his kind, Iulianus was not impressed, but knew that the creature would take orders well, once she had broken him to her will.

He suspected that she was actually looking forward to the job, from the way she smiled and carried herself.

They sipped their drinks in companionable silence for a bit, eying each other like gladiators waiting for the next random draw to see who would fight next.

"My mission in Wildspace has changed, Captain," she addressed herself to the M'Rai as Iulianus watched with Dominion patience. "I will still be hunting Valentinian Tarasicodissa and his crew, but the time has drawn nigh for me to change vessels. *Dominion-427* will be sent home, while I and some of the crew will remain behind."

Iulianus was expecting more of a reaction from the captain, so he couldn't tell if the beast was already drunk or drugged beforehand, or just so nervous that he wouldn't react to any provocation.

Perhaps he had understood the significance of Dominion Security troopers in the corners, after all?

Instead, he nodded, slowly, like he was afraid his head would fall off if he wasn't careful.

"Going forward, I must make plans, but I need some level of interest and commitment from you, Butler Vidy-Wooders," she intoned like a church deacon calling the cadence of a prayer.

"Me?"

She had surprised him. Probably not that hard to do, but then, the man was probably growing desperate as his condition deteriorated, and captains and crews shared the tales of life under the M'Rai captain.

"It is my intention to commission or purchase a warship at Chatosig, Captain Vidy-Wooders," Athanasia ground on, turning wheat kernels to flour beneath her wheels. "Before I do so, I wish to know if I should plan for three meter decks, or four."

Even he was bright enough to catch her meaning now. She was offering him a job, a lifeline perhaps, since the kinds of crews he would be able to hire in the future were going to be more and more the dregs.

Was it worth it, my friend?

"That would involve me selling *Hard Bargain*, yes?" he asked. "If I joined you?"

Oh, my. You're even smarter than a goat, aren't you?

"Most likely," Athanasia hedged. "I expect to be chasing the man hard through warpspace, and *Longshot Hypothesis* is already too fast for almost anything but a dedicated courier. Even *Dominion-427* cannot keep up, but it was never designed for speed. Only my comfort."

Iulianus liked the way the implications of Athanasia's needs seemed to send a hot needle through the man's flesh. Stephaneria had ended up opposite Iulianus, on the far corner of the square. Her fleeting grin spoke volumes as well.

But Athanasia was a senior power of the Dominion, or at least had been until events conspired. That she could play a barbarian like Butler Vidy-Wooders as if he was a violin was almost a given.

"I will need speed and power, Butler," she continued, oozing a sensuality over her words like frosting glazing a piece of fruit. "And people whose rage equals mine, so that they will serve me as we seek our vengeance."

Iulianus was used to suppressing all external emotion in public, especially around the Ambassadors he transported. Athanasia was stroking parts of the man's mind and ego he probably didn't even know he had, truth be told. The Librarian had managed to turn herself in the chair in such a way that she almost appeared to be offering herself to the M'Rai, daring the brute to ravish her, without ever doing one thing that would actually invite it.

Iulianus wondered what either of them would be like in the privacy of a sleeping chamber. Or across the sofa in her personal suite. He would probably find out at some point, so Iulianus made a note to have exterminators come in and spray everything regularly for bugs and whatever else the M'Rai might unknowingly carry with him.

Lice came to mind.

Butler Vidy-Wooders seemed to be having problems breathing.

"I need a hunter," Athanasia let the words dangle in front of the man like a carrot on a long pole. "A tracker. Someone who knows their way around and can teach me things."

Iulianus kept the derisive snort inside as he watched the Widow seduce the fool with her words.

"An officer who can focus on hounding Valentinian Tarasicodissa to the ends of the galaxy, without having to stand watch shifts or do maintenance," she said. "Leaving him time for other endeavors, as I might need things done."

Iulianus was just glad that he hadn't eaten

anything recently, as the thought of that M'Rai rutting with one of the two women, or perhaps both of them at once, so they at least achieved orgasm along the way, didn't cause him to be queasy now.

He had looked up the genetic specifics of the M'Rai in a medical database, when they updated it for Variant Humanities, at the time Stephaneria came aboard. Athanasia could easily fornicate with the giant, as they had been designed to be compatible with species half their size. That just told Iulianus that his own cock was probably bigger than the M'Rai's.

"Officer?" the man rather gasped.

"At the very least," she purred triumphantly. "I won't know how the actual crew will break down until we get closer to having a ship. You may have even more important duties when we get there."

Iulianus grinned inside at the way the fool perked up at the thought of *other duties*. Probably had to pay the station whores extra already, and that would just go up if he had any sort of reputation for brutality around them, as well. Might be too cheap to actually pay that price until his needs got out of hand.

That would just make a man like Butler Vidy-Wooders that much easier to control, if that was the leash the Widow chose to employ.

Iulianus's price wouldn't be anything so mundane.

[20]

GLAXU

GLAXU HAD to give them credit for trying. Or something.

Instead of sending the human captain over to invite him into their conversation, they had sent the extra female. The one that wasn't a sailor in uniform, and didn't move like an assassin. Were they trying to seduce him or something equally detestable?

He wasn't a good judge of age, but Glaxu would have placed her younger than the Widow by a reasonable amount, but still a decade or more older than Bayjy or Kyriaki.

A rose past the bloom, to quote one of his favorite playwrights from the old days. Still equipped with thorns, but no longer attracting the insects to come pollinate her.

Or whatever euphemism the humans might use.

Glaxu was at his prescribed corner of the bar, while the rest of the humans tended to follow a gravity field that pulled them to the far end of the room, leaving him a wide berth to drink his juice properly hot. And the bartender had even left notes or something, because the new one today, a surly-enough near-human, had just nodded and gotten to work.

Glaxu would have left her a spare coin in thanks anyway, even if it wasn't the money Leader had apparently won in a game of cards, funding their excursions yet.

The excess Dominion female approached as the rest settled at the same table they had had earlier. Hilariously, the listening device still worked, but the chair where it was attached had been moved back to the next table over, where a fat, squat Viddhu was eating soup noisily when Glaxu had checked his earphones.

"Captain Redtip?" she said as she approached to a point Dave probably could have predicted with a ruler before she entered.

She was not a killer. At least not as he understood the term. Not like the human Athanasia. Taller than the blond woman. Leaner as well, more in line with the sorts of streamlining a Mondi like him preferred. Brownish head hair a little darker than his feathers, drawn up in a complex, asymmetrical braid showing no gray at all, in spite of her apparent age, so Glaxu assumed a chemical camouflage that he couldn't smell from here.

He hadn't rotated his body as she had approached. Merely drawn his pistol on the hidden site and turned his head.

"Indeed," he nodded politely with a slight head cock.

She had done nothing to warrant rudeness.

Technically none of them had, and it never cost you anything to be polite to people.

Even if you did have to kill them later.

"Athanasia inquires if you would have an interest in joining our group for a common meal, to discuss business," the woman intoned in a quiet, careful voice, standing mostly still, but not so calm as an assassin preparing.

Well done, too. Nothing anyone could take offense at, unless they were already there to begin with. And already part of the plan as they had hatched it at that table after he had left the other day.

Seriously? You think a mere triple-cross will be sufficient to cheat a Mondi?

"I will join," Glaxu nodded to her with dignity, letting his head crest semaphore courtesy and grace as he holstered the pistol, grabbed his juice, and stepped off the bar stool.

The woman waited patiently, and then rotated in place to lead him back to the table, as if a herald.

Glaxu took a moment to study today's companions in greater detail than he had as they made their way through the room.

Athanasia. The Widow of not-Dave-Hall, dressed in a tighter outfit than yesterday, with a tunic to only mid-thigh instead of her ankles, and wrapping her like a second skin. Gray, as the previous one had been, two days ago, but a darker shade, down in the steel and charcoal range. Suggestions of evil and power, if he understood the human hints, mixed with sex and rage.

Glaxu hoped the silly woman wasn't planning to seduce him. He doubted she had the correct internal spiraling for the act, even if he could have found the interest.

The other woman took her spot across from the Widow, leaving an empty chair on the end of the oval.

The human ship captain from before sat diagonal from Athanasia, prim and specist in his haughtiness. Pressed and impeccable in the rest.

The fourth made Glaxu happy that he couldn't grin outwardly. And that he could contain his mirth before it reached his head feathers.

Leader and Fierce Bayjy had shown him a picture of Butler Vidy-Wooders, the captain of Bayjy's former employment, *Hard Bargain*.

M'Rai were certainly impressive creatures. Three times Glaxu's height. Easily eight to ten times his mass.

It was probably a dreadful oversight on his part that he had forgotten to put on the shock bracers this afternoon before he went out for an evening's entertainment. If trouble erupted, he would have no choice but to dewclaw some stupid bastard.

Even more interestingly, the creature on display here was quite different from his old pictures. The facial hair had been trimmed back to a level that might have made a different man look distinguished. The head hair appeared brushed back and tied into a ribbon or something, rather than the unruly madness he had apparently normally preferred.

Introductions, more formal this time. Stephaneria was the extra female. Glaxu still could not place her purpose in this nest. He wondered if they had brought along a sex-object, but he could not for the life of him understand why she might be important enough to dine with the elders of that nest.

Glaxu did make carefully sure not to react to Bayjy's nemesis, Butler. Or perhaps she and Kyriaki were Vidy-Wooders's nemesis. Those stories had left him rolling on the floor in a fit of giggles and feathers.

"So, Captain Redtip," the Widow said after they had ordered food and drink. "What loyalties do you have to your former shipmates?"

It took him a moment, as his mind kept flashing back to the old nest of Mondi that had assumed he had remained behind, as he had wished, when he had merely been stranded by an Overdrive failure. But she meant Leader, Bayjy, Kyriaki, and not-Dave-Hall.

"I'm here, they have left," he shrugged, somehow failing to mention that it was part of a larger plan that they *left him behind*, rather than a *parting of the ideological ways*.

"But you know where they intended to transit to next?" she asked in a light, friendly tone.

Two old friends, well met and gossiping about old shipmates. Or some such drivel.

"I was privy to their plans, right up until they hit the buoys, madam," he suggested off-handedly. "If they truly maintained course, then yes."

"I would like to invest in your knowledge," she said.

What an interesting play on words, even for humans.

"Oh?" he decided to play adroitly stupid.

It had worked wonders with Truqtok's people. It might work here, although this group was far more dangerous than most of the folk he had met on Kryuome.

"Captain Vidy-Wooders here has decided to join my vengeance," she smiled, reaching out and even stroking the M'Rai on the arm in a manner that Glaxu's interspecies erotica studies had suggested human women didn't normally do with strangers, or even close acquaintances.

But then, M'Rai were probably human enough.

"Then you probably don't need me," Glaxu smiled at her serenely.

"Need?" she smiled politely back. "Perhaps not. Desire your assistance. And would be willing to recompense you for your time."

"And none of the fixers, fences, or other whores on the station were able to guide the next leg of your journey?"

Glaxu let his eyes grow large as he spoke. Among Mondi, that improved near-distance accuracy on a beak strike, but to humans, it apparently looked like surprised innocence, from what he had been told.

Too bad none of you knew that.

The two captains appeared to deflate just a little, while the two women retained their calm dignity. But then, the other two human women he had known, Bayjy and Kyriaki, were probably more dangerous than the men, at least within their realms of expertise.

"Captain Tarasicodissa might have mentioned things to folks, but the man has a reputation with misdirection that I have come to appreciate and respect," Athanasia tutted.

"So you didn't find a secret, hidden, Urlan base at the south pole, either?" Glaxu chuckled happily.

Leader had certainly ruffled everyone else's feathers with that one.

"We looked among the prospectors," she joined his mirth with a laugh. A moment later, the others did as well. "But were unable to locate our prey. We came here for other reasons, and managed to get lucky enough to find you, apparently bereft."

"Merchants are dull folks," Glaxu offered, not bothering to point out that Valentinian and friends had reinvented themselves as salvagers, at least until they could return to more profitable ventures later, when *Dominion-427* was no longer hunting them.

"Just so," Athanasia smiled. "But we will no longer be merely chasing the ship across the galaxy."

"Oh?" Glaxu let himself perk up.

This might be actionable intelligence that would justify blowing his cover and fleeing to warn his nest.

"*Dominion-427* was only on loan," her voice got harder and sharper as she spoke. "I have sufficient funds at hand to detach myself from the ship, buy a new one, and pursue other ventures as well."

Glaxu nodded serenely as he kept his head crest elevated by sheer force of will.

"Chatosig is a notable destination for someone interested in such activities," he said, turning his attention directly on the until-now-silent M'Rai. "Are you part of her new squadron of pursuers, Captain?"

For a man who liked to play poker for money, Butler Vidy-Wooders did not have an especially bland face. He almost looked like the other captain had silently kicked him under the table, from the way he flinched.

The giant cleared his throat and glanced at the

Widow like he was asking permission to speak. Interesting. Even more so when the woman nodded.

"*Hard Bargain* has been a good ship for me," the man said carefully. "But times have changed, and I will sell it and put the money in the bank. With other funds already invested, it will generate interest for the time being, until I have destroyed Tarasicodissa and Endon. After that, I will look for my next venture."

Glaxu knew he shouldn't have been shocked. Bayjy had told her tale of woe. And the one of vengeance that more than balanced the scales. Personally, Glaxu was more surprised that the man was smart enough to get out now, but he supposed that the Widow had thrown him a lifesuit in impending vacuum, and he had taken it rather than explode in space.

Glaxu nodded his attention back to the Widow.

"Commissioning a warship at M'Rai physical scales will take time," he said socially. "I cannot imagine *Longshot Hypothesis* will remain in dock while you delay."

"Fortunately, there already exists such a vessel," she smiled at him with great innocence, for a human. "Somewhat old, but capable of being refurbished and upgraded in a relatively short period of time. A dealer at Chatosig-One, of all places, had it for sale. They had bought it from a M'Rai pirate some time back, but were unable to sell it later, as one of the periodic wars and tides shifted through and most of the local M'Rai migrated to other sectors of space. At least the more criminal element that needed such a warship."

"Interesting," Glaxu nodded. "I wasn't aware that

there were enough M'Rai in the area to make up a crew."

"There aren't any more," she leaned forward just a little. Possibly a human gesture women used to distract men, from the unconscious way she seemed to display her upper chest to him and the effect similar motions by Bayjy or Kyriaki had on the two human males. "But the necessary refits and updates to convert it to a human standard crew, while expensive, aren't that much more than fixing it up for the M'Rai."

"Does it come with a shuttle bay?" Glaxu asked, jutting his beak out just a little to sell his interest.

And he confused her, just for a moment, as something clouded her eyes before vanishing. She turned her attention off to the other captain, Palaiologos.

"It does not," he spoke up quickly. "At least in the current configuration midship. This was designed originally as an escort for one of the small navies some of the local kingdoms build when they want to conquer a neighbor or three. There is a storage area just inward of a large cargo airlock, that could be converted to a flight deck, but nothing as big as a Mondi-sized, variable geometry slayership could fit right now."

"Would you be interested in hiring an escort ship?" he ventured.

What was the worst they could do? Offer?

And him? Accept?

"I hadn't anticipated that your services might be on the market, Captain Redtip," Athanasia tried to recover things.

Glaxu shrugged.

"My original nest has returned home, or at least headed towards the homeward sectors," he said honestly. "I'm at Chatosig, having escaped from Kryuome instead of continuing to be stranded, or gotten myself killed. I need to start looking at future employment options soon."

"You were stranded at Kryuome?" the other female, Stephaneria, spoke up suddenly.

He had almost forgotten she was there, quiet as a snake hiding in the grass from a hungry Mondi.

Her eyes were sharper now, commensurate with a hidden intellect that could explain her presence with this group.

"Overdrive failure," he nodded to her. "I was separated from my old nest and they assumed I had stayed behind. Captain Tarasicodissa hired me to help him kill some of the local gangsters that had been causing problems. Part of the payment was parts and expertise to rebuild my own systems. We both flew as far as Chatosig, him looking for the next cargo, me looking for the next raid that someone needed to hire muscle for."

There. Almost a real truth, depending on how you wanted to look at it.

Something rather interesting passed between the two women's eyes. Glaxu didn't have the body language down to do more than rate the importance and excitement of the look, but it was there. All the emotions at the table changed in a heartbeat.

It was enough difference that he loosened up his legs from the squat he had assumed earlier and flexed his toes outward against the plastic, pseudo-wood of the chair. Never knew when you should prepare to suddenly explode upwards on madly-flapping wings, striking every direction with dewclaws while you drew your pistol and cut loose.

After a moment, calmness returned, and Glaxu wondered if he had just cut a significant portion of Vidy-Wooders's net value to the women by possibly being available to hire.

Not that they could afford Redtip Windrunner Oedressa *Farther* Glaxu, but these people were a threat to his new nest. Anything he could do to damage their peace of mind would help.

He just wasn't suicidal enough to kill everyone here and then try his luck with the authorities on-station.

"That is certainly an interesting and unexpected development, Captain Redtip," Athanasia said after a moment to clear her flutters.

Glaxu invested everything he had into the most nonchalant shrug he could manage. Difficult when you didn't really have shoulders. Elbows had to make up for it.

"As I said, at some point, I will need something else," he said evenly. "Even parked in the cheap section of the station and watching my coin carefully, I will run out of funds at some point not too distant."

Translation into human: I'm not broke. How desperate are you?

The Widow nodded as a way of closing off that portion of the conversation, and then shifted seamlessly into talk about station politics and other sundries of almost no relevance at all, except to distract everyone from the one cogent point, or perhaps two, that had come up. The Mondi could be for rent. The Widow was buying a second-hand M'Rai light corvette, if it was the one he had scanned earlier, and would be chasing Valentinian with more help. Local help.

Glaxu enjoyed his steak strips, cut to mimic grilled snake, if a little bland and chewy with cartilage. Nothing else important happened. Dessert was skipped for more coffee for the humans and juice for him.

Stephaneria had gone mostly silent. Captain Palaiologos had responded to technical questions with precise answers. Vidy-Wooders looked like a stiff drink would help.

The Widow kept all sides talking, like a dancer at the center of a scrum until they broke back into two groups and Glaxu found himself headed back to *Outermost* with serious, personal concern.

Not tonight, but how soon should he break cover and run for Leader with the updated information the man needed to make better plans? Enough to confirm the hull? The upgrades?

Dare he actually listen to the employment offer that would no doubt require an internal conversion on their part?

Butler Vidy-Wooders might not even be necessary, if Redtip was available. That was part of the look he had seen floating between the two women. The human captain had given nothing away, while the M'Rai was an open book nobody had bothered to write anything in.

Perhaps the Widow wasn't as foolish as he had expected?

At least the game ahead would be entertaining.

It had been a long time since Glaxu had known a worthy opponent.

[21]

ATHANASIA

"Thoughts?" Athanasia asked as she reclined on the sofa in her salon.

Stephaneria remained with her, once she had sent the two men to their stations. Iulianus was at least close at hand if she felt ready to trigger the confrontation that would bind that man to her.

Or alienate her one, truly dangerous ally.

The Librarian was preparing stronger drinks than they had allowed themselves earlier.

"Landing the Mondi is a coup that perhaps eliminates the need for the M'Rai," Stephaneria said carefully. "Or reduces the man to a bulldog you can sic on Tarasicodissa to maul him to death."

"But?" Athanasia heard the tones in her pupil's voice.

"I find the setting to be too coincidental," Stephaneria continued. "Yes, the bird could have flown here in tandem with *Longshot Hypothesis*, when our target fled Kryuome, and then fallen out later. If I wanted to plant a mole in your organization, or a trap, it would look remarkably like that."

"And yet, we cannot know," Athanasia concluded the thought. "Certainly, I would not want to build the Mondi a flight deck and allow him aboard this ship if I wasn't sure about his loyalties, but there is no way to test that now."

She watched Stephaneria with undisguised appreciation as the woman approached. The librarian had reinvented herself completely under Athanasia's touch. Transformed herself into a younger version of the Widow, plagued by the same fires and rage that could only be quenched in the blood of two men that would be taken together.

Athanasia accepted one glass and watched Stephaneria curl her legs under her on the floor at her master's feet, leaning lightly against Athanasia's leg for warmth and comfort.

"I am inclined to keep Vidy-Wooders in harness," Athanasia decided after a gulp of the stiff drink. "Redtip can be hired for flying muscle, as he offered. We just won't tell him anything more than we would any other mercenary thug we brought aboard. If Tarasicodissa hasn't sold *Longshot Hypothesis* by now, he most likely won't because Chatosig is one of the best places in Wildspace to make such a trade, at least according to our M'Rai and a few others I have investigated."

"And if he escapes us?" Stephaneria's tones had a dark current that ran under them. The kind that warmed Athanasia's soul to hear.

"When we own a few planets, or pirate strongholds, we'll just put out a bounty on the men that's high enough to draw in the right sort of folks to claim it," she purred. "When you have planetary budgets to play with, such funds become rounding errors, while at the same time more money than most of those killers make in a decade."

"So we might not kill them ourselves, but we'll still be delivered the heads?" the Librarian turned and looked up at her like a newly hatched bird looking for a meal.

"Indeed, my dear," Athanasia reached down a hand to run it through Stephaneria's hair, luxuriating in the feel and the purrs that emanated from the woman.

It could all still be a trap. She had no way short of betrayal by the little birdman to determine, at least until they had *Longshot Hypothesis* under their guns and she watched the Mondi annihilate the transport for her.

Or if he tried to stop her, and she had him splattered across space.

The new vessel was a purpose-built warship, designed and built by a species of berserker warriors for their specific needs, rather than an armed courier intended for transporting high lords and ambassadors in comfort. Even the Mondi's slayership wouldn't be able to do more than irritate her before he died.

In fact, she almost hoped that Redtip did betray her at the end, just so she could see how well his kind went against her, in case she needed to perhaps conquer a few of those sectors, or perhaps recruit squadrons of his kind to serve her.

Athanasia planned to become a Queen before she

was done. Whatever men had to die now, or later, would just serve that purpose.

And she could include birdmen in the cause.

[22]
VALENTINIAN

HE HAD NEVER REALLY BEEN a reader, but it turned out to be a good way to escape the others for a few hours after dinner. Valentinian had only had Artaxerxes as crew before, and keeping a ship in tune kept them out of each other's hair most of the time.

Now, he had three others, instead of just the one, and they were all contributing to maintenance, so things got done quickly. Plus, he had been spending five to eight hours a day around everyone, more than half of it with the gravity turned off so they could get the big beams welded into place and then put down solid decks.

Bayjy had pronounced herself satisfied with the results today. Everything would hold weight even in landing maneuvers. Tomorrow, they could start running ducts for power, water, and air while leaving the gravity on all the time again.

Valentinian hadn't bothered with purchasing hatches and such yet. They would get the space enclosed and then could add in walls to break things up. Closing off doorways would be the last thing they did before they called it good.

So he was forward, down in his own cabin. Dinner had been exciting, as they all realized how far they had come, but he was tired of people right now. Close the hatch, stretch out on the rack, turn on the overhead lamp.

He had picked up this book from Marduk when they first hit Kryuome. At the time, Valentinian had been looking for a way to baseline the surface of a planet that had been knocked a little sideways in its orbit by someone mad enough to throw a small moon at it. He hadn't been able to read the Urlan hardly at all, but Bayjy had found a translation guide for him, so he had spent the last few weeks working on understanding more than just the maps.

It helped that most written languages these days had descended from Urlan, so he could frequently sound something out and make sense of it.

Valentinian sat bolt upright in surprise, numbly happy that his bunk wasn't tucked into a small space on the wall, or he would have bashed his head against something. He went back and reread several paragraphs to make sure that he had not misinterpreted or mistranslated.

Nope. Shit. Maybe. I don't know.

He didn't bother with shoes. His socks were good enough for now, and the ship was warmer than he liked to keep it, so he didn't need a jacket inside like he used to.

Valentinian emerged from his cabin with the book in one hand. He and Dave's rec room downstairs was normally the crew space, when he was carrying passengers, but that had gotten a little awkward with

Kyriaki and Bayjy taking up the two cabins above him. Another reason they were adding more space aft.

He went up the four steps into the main corridor, turned, and walked up the stairwell, following the pivot midway. He never took the elevator, unless he had something too heavy to carry, like frozen food boxes for the kitchen.

Upstairs, nobody was in the kitchen area, so he looked into the lounge to port-side and found Dave watching something on the big wall screen. Looked like a kid's cartoon, except that everything was in a language Valentinian didn't speak. Wasn't Urlan, so he wasn't interested in learning it today. He crossed back to starboard, where the two women bunked.

Both doors were closed. Hopefully Bayjy was still awake, because he didn't want to leave this until breakfast if she was. Valentinian rapped on her hatch with the back of his knuckles. A moment later she opened it.

Bayjy was Pranai. A little taller than him. Broader in the shoulders and hips. Stronger. Probably outweighed him, but that wasn't a question you asked a woman. Skin a little darker than lavender, but not purple, except in the right light. Bald, but a perfectly shaped skull.

Her kind had been engineered for hot planets. Places where the temperature was over thirty degrees at night, and might get up to fifty during the day. Even keeping *Longshot Hypothesis* five degrees warmer than normal didn't really impress her. Instead, she wore her heatsuit almost all the time.

It was a compact spacesuit, depending on how you wanted to look at it. Covered her to wrists and ankles and neck and kept her body temperature high enough that she was comfortable. It also fit her like a second skin, which was why she normally wore clothing over it. Wasn't technically necessary, except for the effect that her clad nudity had on other people.

Like Valentinian.

"Got needs tonight, Captain?" she asked with a lascivious grin and a twinkle in her eyes as she stood in the doorway. That heatsuit didn't really leave anything important to the imagination.

He hadn't touched Kyriaki. He hadn't touched Bayjy. Hell, he hadn't even touched that librarian back on Bohrne Station, Stephaneria. He couldn't see a positive outcome to any of those encounters in the long run.

Wasn't going to try finding one. He had enough craziness in his life without it, thank you very much.

Valentinian held out the book like it was a stake that might keep a vampire at bay. His finger still marked the spot.

"Read this page," he said as she took the book from his hand. "Then put some clothes on and join me in the wardroom in a few minutes."

He could have made it sound like a request, but his head really wasn't there right now. Instead, he stepped back, nodded, and walked away.

Kyriaki was standing in her doorway when he passed. She was still fully dressed, which happened to include an oversized dark blue Henley shirt that had vanished out of his trunk at some point.

"News?" she asked simply as he approached.

"Maybe nothing but paranoia," he offered, but didn't stop walking.

Somehow, he wasn't surprised when she emerged in his wake. Dave was standing in the doorway from the kitchen when Valentinian stepped into the lounge.

"What?" Valentinian demanded in a quiet tone.

"Look on your face, young man," Dave replied with deadly seriousness. "Can't be good."

"Whatever it is has been dead for two thousand years," Valentinian replied tiredly. "And I'm reasonably confident that it's still there."

"What is?"

Kyriaki had joined him, so Valentinian pulled out a chair against the magnets holding it in place, and plopped down on it. Dave ended up across the table, and Kyriaki left a seat between them.

Valentinian grimaced, tried to make it look like a smile, and sat, stewing in his juices. Dead silent.

The other two joined him.

"Holy shit, Vee," Bayjy came barging into the room, book in one hand. At least she had taken a moment to pull on pants and a baggy enough shirt.

Small victories.

Valentinian smiled as Bayjy clattered to a halt, surprised to find everyone waiting for her. Rather than sit right next to him on either side, she apparently decided to play it safe and ended up one down from Dave. She took a deep breath and laid the book open between them, spinning it around so the words pointed at him.

"One: how the hell did nobody notice this until now?" she demanded. "Two: did they strip the place in the ancient era and then close it back up afterwards?"

Valentinian shrugged.

"I would expect…something," he said. "The muties certainly don't know what's under their feet. Not if they're praying facing the other direction."

"Uhm, question?" Kyriaki spoke up. "What the hell are you two talking about?"

Valentinian forced himself to take a breath. Deep and slow. Presumably calming, but his heart was racing right now.

"I bought the book because I needed maps to get us to the site where the treasure map pointed," he said simply. Slowly. Almost painfully. "Didn't really read it all that close other than that, because I still don't read Urlan that well. Teaching myself, so I can help Bayjy with research going forward, since she's already fluent."

"Still not making sense," Kyriaki tapped a finger on the tabletop at him like a mother with a recalcitrant child.

"Kryuome was a sector capital when the war broke out," Valentinian refused to be hurried right now. "Big naval bases in orbit, and a few on the ground. You can plot those by the radiation signatures where the human armies dropped the biggest, nastiest nuclear bombs that they could make onto ground targets. Then they deorbited the stations. From the descriptions in another chapter, they didn't bother evacuating them first, just shot them to pieces and watched those burn in the atmosphere. Except most of the pieces were too big to burn up, so they hit the ground. Then the fleets somehow hit the place with a small moon. Or a bunch of them. That story's largely apocryphal, I think."

"Got it," Kyriaki nodded. "Serious orbital bombardment. Why are you fidgeting?"

"The treasure map is not in Urlan," Valentinian replied. "I'm guessing prisoners told prisoners. Fathers told daughters. That sort of thing. Eventually, someone wrote it down. Maybe several times, but I've got no clue right now, and won't until we get back there and open the place up with Dave's new key he built."

"What's there, Vee?" Dave asked in a calming, quieting voice that Valentinian really appreciated right now.

"Those remains are, were, the city of T'Ilard," Valentinian said. "More specifically, an Imperial hunting lodge and palace, on the shores of a lake that used to exist there before the place dried up."

"That basin was a lake?" Kyriaki asked, turning back and forth between him and Bayjy.

"A humungous, enormous lake," Bayjy said. "Two hundred kilometers long and forty wide. Pretty shallow, but a lovely, blue thing surrounded by an emerald paradise, once upon a time. Vee, you think the T'Brask are the descendants of the city dwellers? We know they aren't Urlan."

"T'Brask?" Kyriaki asked.

"The muties Basuk was talking about," Valentinian said. "The desert folk who still return to those remains, in spite of the place being too hot with radiation for people to survive there longer than a little while, even with good medicine."

"So we might have an Urlan palace to loot?" Dave whistled.

"No, that was destroyed," Bayjy said. "One of the

nukes was dropped right on top of it and exploded at low level like a bulldozer."

"So what are we looking at here?" Kyriaki asked.

"An Urlan military depot if I read that right," Valentinian replied. "And maybe the place they stored things too valuable to keep out in the palace itself where any servant could just steal them."

"Oh, shit," Kyriaki whispered. "And you think it's still there?"

"I don't think you can close up the vault door we found without some specialized tools," Bayjy said. "That was an old Urlan trick, to keep you from hiding that you had stolen anything. One of the reasons we tend to cut through bulkheads, since important doors tend to do stupid things when you don't open them with the right key."

"Do we know what's actually down there?" Dave asked.

"No," Valentinian said. "Could be anything, considering the state of the craziness just before the human fleets arrived to bomb everything. But whatever it is has most certainly been there for two thousand years."

[23]
IULIANUS

As vessels went, Iulianus wasn't all that impressed by the aesthetics. The spaciousness wasn't all that different from *Dominion-427*, but the courier was designed to be open and airy, since it wasn't expected to look for trouble, merely to shoot its way out. The old M'Rai ship had probably felt a little cramped to them, even with ceilings that tended to be four meters high.

It was the brutalism of the naval architecture that offended him, if he had to put too fine a point on it. Dominion warships were generally sleek and elegant, inside and out, with long curves and sweeping lines uninterrupted by anything.

This ship reminded Iulianus of a series of boxes welded together in spacedock. Cubes of varying sizes, with the largest ones running in parallel lines down the spine and both flanks, with smaller ones in between. From above or below, the hull of the ship looked vaguely like a blanket that had been pressed together to create three, linear folds.

But even then, the builders hadn't bothered with the extra step of smoothing out the ripples, so it was a set of steps up and down. With antennae attached apparently at random.

The edges of the ship stepped back up again to house three turret emplacements on each side. Light ones, designed to pummel small craft like that Mondi's fightership, or a transport like *Longshot Hypothesis*. Centerline, fore and aft, top deck and bottom, were four heavier turrets, the kind designed to engage other ships in this class.

A team of such ships might have been assigned to escort something like a Dominion ZoneWatcher into battle, or maybe a ZoneStriker. Even a pack of such ships wouldn't last very long against a line of SkyStrikers by themselves.

Luckily, nobody but the Dominion had such formidable vessels, at least as far as Iulianus had been able to determine. If the Widow was intent on conquering a few planets in Wildspace and carving out a pocket empire for herself, this hull would be an adequate starting point.

At least until they needed to commission one of the yards at someplace like Chatosig-Five to build them something the next scale larger.

Iulianus wondered how much trouble could he get into, if he could eventually build a SkyWatcher-sized ship, and recruit several divisions of M'Rai instead of the Dominion's Caelon Assault Cavalry.

Like so many of the Variant Humanities, M'Rai had no homeworld. None that had survived the ancient revolt that broke the Urlan and destroyed so many of the overlords' planets, at least. You found various folks mixed in with other mongrels on the

Wildspace planets and stations, perhaps clustered in obscure tribes. Nowhere that the Widow could just appear with money and adventure and recruit herself an army.

Still, it was an impressive ship. Expensive to update and maintain, as none of the systems around here had been organized enough to support such a vessel for perhaps the fifty years since it had been laid up. Workers had already been through the bridge, as he looked around him and considered his future.

The Widow was waiting patiently to one side, with her Librarian at hand. Vidy-Wooders was putting his expertise to use aft, working with local crews on one of the gun stations. It had been built for a M'Rai, so he could answer questions as the smaller humans rebuilt the gunnery stations for the rest of the galaxy to use.

So they were alone in this chamber. Him and the two women, both patiently waiting and watching. He turned to them now, aware that all his prevarications and delays had finally reached that point where the hangman was preparing the noose for his neck.

Her smile was a sufficient window into her soul.

"Iulianus?" she asked pleasantly, surprising him that she would use the personal name in company.

But then, the Librarian wasn't really a separate entity anymore, was she? Just an extension of the Widow's need and rage.

As are we all.

"Athanasia," he replied, watching the third person blink suddenly in barely-covered surprise.

But Stephaneria was Laurentian. Didn't really

understand Dominion culture and social mores in a visceral way, down in the blood. To her, it was just data to be absorbed, stored, and retransmitted as information later.

"You have put me off as long as you could," the Widow said with a serious, deadly smile. "Tell me about your secret orders. The ones you received from the Solar Party, transmitted directly to you by the Lord of the Dominion Armada himself."

Yes, she would have known the bureaucratic process well enough to predict the flow of that stream, from the cold, mountain glaciers down to the sea.

Again, the quick glance at Stephaneria. More of a reflex than anything. He had been stealing himself to open as much of his soul as was necessary with this woman.

He just hadn't expected the Widow to make a burlesque of it.

"She's mine," Athanasia said. "Body and soul. Just as you will be soon."

Images of praying mantises flashed before Iulianus. At least she was an attractive woman, one who worked endlessly at her training, that she could be perhaps a decade and a half older than him and in better shape than most of the women he had ever known, regardless of age.

Iulianus nodded, mostly to himself.

"They wish you to never return to Dominion space," he said simply. "My orders were to do whatever it took to prevent you crossing that line inward. Whatever chase. Whatever subterfuges."

"Whatever assassinations?" her eyes mocked him now.

As he knew they would.

"If you took it into your mind that you could return, victorious or not, I was to stop you," Iulianus said simply.

Both women nodded, in harmony. It was eerie.

"And if I remain in Wildspace, Iulianus?" the Widow asked. "What then?"

"To encourage whatever whims kept you here. Keep you here," he replied evenly. Carefully. "To serve them, even, if that would help."

"So you cannot return home either?" her smile turned feral.

"No," he acknowledged. "Not while you live. And certainly not while your own mission remains unfulfilled."

"Then you are already mine," she crooned.

"Who is Dave Hall?" Iulianus countered.

He might serve, but he was not a servant. He could settle for being a junior partner, perhaps, like Stephaneria, suborned to the greater mission, but he would sit at the high table.

"My husband," Athanasia replied automatically. Her eyes grew serious and shrewd now as she realized the negotiations had only just begun.

"Who was he before this?" Iulianus pressed, noting absently that the librarian had rotated her body inward some, so that now she was more off to one side, rather than merely standing at the Widow's shoulder. "What makes Dave Hall so important?"

She paused, and Iulianus knew he had struck close to home.

"If I tell you, you can never go home, Iulianus," she said after a moment. "Even with my head in a bag."

"You ask me to carry my orders out to the logical extreme, Athanasia," he replied. "To commit to your conspiracy with my soul. You can do the same, if you wish me to remain as your partner. If I stay, many others will as well, convinced that this is both a grand adventure, as well as something their orders from the Dominion Armada demand of them."

"I will own you," she said simply.

"You own me now," he said sharply. "But let us discard our old masks and have this out in the open. If we are to disregard the Dominion, then their ways must be reviewed, and perhaps disregarded as well. My treason will not come cheap, Athanasia."

"Nor should it, Iulianus," she smiled. "If it did, then I would never trust it."

He nodded, acknowledging this truth. The Dominion was a land of masks, even in private. Only the Dominion Armada did without them, separated from the other forces in that particular way. The Dominator's Caelon Assault Cavalry. The Solar Guard. The other land and space troops.

Everyone wore a mask. An officer of the Dominion Armada just didn't make his with plastic and steel.

"So what will it be, Athanasia?" he asked bitterly. "Which treason will you choose?"

Part of his mind registered that Stephaneria seemed to be breathing heavily, as if sexually aroused. He didn't want to dwell on the implications of that. Not today.

No good would come of it.

Athanasia surprised him utterly by reaching down and pulling her tight, gray tunic up and over her head, casting it with great accuracy into the chair where the ship's captain would sit when the vessel was in commission.

Underneath, she wore a semi-armored bustier in a light gray. He could see plates and lines in the fabric, indicating where armor protected her breasts and stomach, almost like a loose corset.

Hooks kept it together. Twelve of them as she undid each, starting at the top, before tossing it onto her top. Athanasia stood topless before him, medium-sized breasts still firm in spite of her age.

Iulianus remained frozen, an alabaster statue. Perhaps Medusa's latest victim.

"I will have the greatest treason out of you, Iulianus Palaiologos," the Widow smiled as she stepped close.

Her left hand grasped his right and placed it on her breast. He could feel her excitement, her hammering heartbeat through her skin. Feel it in her nipple, protruding like a cut diamond.

"Dave Hall had another life once," she whispered, close enough now that he could lean down a little and kiss her, if he dared. "Another face."

"Before he assassinated the Dominator?" Iulianus pressed.

She looked up at him with a predatory triumph in her eyes. She would have him, right here on this deck, it seemed. Possibly with a witness. Perhaps an assistant, he wasn't sure. But he had asked for treason from them both, so perhaps that was appropriate.

"Dave Hall didn't assassinate the Dominator," her other hand came up and touched his jaw lightly, as if measuring it for a kiss or a blow. "Dave Hall *was* the Dominator."

[24]
GLAXU

HE DECIDED that maybe Leader was right, although Glaxu would never have believed it if he hadn't witnessed it firstfoot. By the time he had returned to *Outermost* and taken a nap, at least three semi-serious job offers had arrived in his message box, from people unrelated to *Dominion-427*, looking to hire a slayership for some task.

Were all these people telepathic? He hadn't talked to anyone. Nobody had been close enough to even look at him while he sat at the bar. Only after the conversation with the Widow.

Glaxu paused mid-rant and wondered if she had told the fixers and fences that she was considering hiring the bird. Had perhaps set her own foot trap and waited for him to wander into it without looking.

Crap. Truly, a devious, masterful maneuver, if she had. Now he would need to spend precious observation time dealing with yahoos and hooligans probably not normally worth his time, just to maintain his cover.

Ambushing the woman and her assistants in a hallway kept sounding more and more rewarding, but that was just the pique talking and he knew it. Hell, she might have done it as an insurance policy, just to see how long she could string him along.

Grumble.

Okay, first one in. Are you kidding me?

Actually, looking at the signature block, they probably weren't. An offer to enter into the lists for a fighting tournament, put on by a human supremacist organization, with the promise of a major purse for the winner. Presumably only humans were allowed to seriously compete.

There were any number of ways to damage a competitor in such a thing without leaving claw prints in the dirt afterwards.

Just to be a shit, he replied, seeking more information. And made a note to wear the shock bracers every time he left the ship after this. Handy to take most humans down, and he had tuned his a little high, just in case a M'Rai came along and needed killing.

He'd deal with those morons if they had the tail feathers to actually engage him in anything more than simian poop-flinging exercises.

Next…

Glaxu read it again. And a third time. Still didn't make a lick of sense, but he couldn't find a flaw in the logic.

Local xenoanthropologist post-doc attempting to assemble a catalog of all the known sentient species in this multi-sector chunk of space, to update the previous catalog that had lain dormant for sixty years.

Huh.

Well, true, Mondi hadn't been here then. Too busy helping put down the Griishu, and after that working for the Bahgh to conquer Verkossin.

Still, Glaxu approached that one with a long toe stuck out. Perhaps it was just the paranoia speaking, but how better to get inside your opponent's head and find his weaknesses than to throw an academic at them, in the name of science?

Maybe he was just too devious, but one could never be too paranoid, especially without a nest watching his pinions.

Finally, the third message looked legitimate. As much as anything on this station had. Standard caravan guard kind of job, from the description. Fly escort for a freighter captain hauling expensive luxury goods around a reasonably fixed ring of systems, rather than bulk cargo or random passengers.

Maybe AND random passengers, but they wouldn't be valuable, unless you knew something ahead of time and then it was a political kidnapping, not a raid.

One should always know the finer details of one's expertise.

All of the planets listed were the harder, sharper type in this part of Wildspace. Much closer in style to Kryuome than Chatosig, which tended to be almost as civilized as the Mondi sectors. Boring, if you will, which was why so many nests decided to head elsewhere and work as mercenaries.

Ozzo the merchant might know more. Glaxu left

his cold weather gear on, sighed and put on the shock bracers, and headed inward to make his way to the bazaar.

Leader had suggested the additional security methods that Glaxu confirmed as he left the ship and activated them. A secondary alarm that could only be disabled from his card-reader, rather than locally.

Plus, it was a Mondi slayership. Glaxu hadn't met any other species in this sector that would be comfortable with narrow, meter-plus-tall hallways, so he doubted anyone would break in.

The docking configuration pulled all three beams in and hid them behind armored panels. Glaxu went ahead and locked those as well. There was no legitimate reason for someone to need to open them, from the inside or out, so that was just one more place where someone trying to do to him what Bayjy and Kyriaki had done to the M'Rai would get his attention.

Outside, the corridor was clear. Rather than run in elegant curves, this station was a series of straight lines connected by shallow angles. Twenty-four faces, seen from above, if he remembered. Outermost ring was dedicated to docks and shipping warehouses.

Inward, the next ring was concentrated on business. Made sense, if you could back your store up against your warehouse, so the outer edge of ring two was for the larger shops, the more successful ones that could afford the prime real estate.

Ozzo's shop was on the inner edge. The less reputable side of the ten-meter-wide hallways. Glaxu approached it from a long ways off, watching for watchers, either paying attention to him or to Ozzo.

There wasn't much he could do about being the

only Mondi currently on station, other than to make sure he meandered a bit when he visited the station, stopping into random shops and poking around.

Never know when you'll find buried treasure, as Bayjy apparently had with Ozzo. Never know when you wanted to confuse spotters.

He even went well past Ozzo's shop today, just so he could stick his beak into a shop that sold gems and polished stones. He didn't have anyone to impress for spring mating, and purchasing something for one of the human women in his nest could be misinterpreted, but he was keeping track of the traffic behind him, more than anything.

So far, so good.

He stepped into Ozzo's shop, making sure to duck below the light beam that sounded a chime. No point in letting someone know where he was, if they had lost sight, was there?

The shopkeeper was tiny for a human, not more than a third taller than Glaxu. The Mondi didn't know the exact subspecies, but he presumed the man was one of the genetically-engineered variants so common in Wildspace.

"Good morning, dangerous hunting bird," Ozzo grinned as he watched Glaxu emerge from the tall shelving. "How may I be of assistance?"

Good, no comment about ducking under the light, which he had to have known about. Perhaps he understood that the situation was more than it appeared yesterday.

"Gossip, more than anything," Glaxu said, moving to the far edge of the counter separating them, so he had a reasonable view of shadows entering the shop. To lubricate things, he added a coin to the pile of papers between the two of them.

"Is unnecessary," the human glanced at the coin and made no effort to reach for it. "Friends of pretty lady Bayjy, regardless of silly stories fools tell each other in shadows."

Glaxu cocked his head each way briefly, trying to read the human's body language. From Bayjy's tales, he was the oldest human she had ever met, tiny and wizened, but still sharp as a dewclaw.

"*Hard Bargain* is in station," Glaxu offered as a thread that they might tug on.

"Is," the merchant agreed. "Another silly fool, but big bastard, so nobody call him that to his face except Bayjy and pretty blond woman. For sale, if you want a mid-range salvage vulture in not-bad-shape. Best that he sell now, since it only break down tomorrow at this rate. Unknown First Mate's estranged mate on station now as well. With gunship and crew. Buying bigger gunship and hiring killers. Mondi need bigger guns?"

"Perhaps, but that's not why I'm here," Glaxu shrugged.

How to explain to a non-Mondi what variable geometry meant. It wasn't just engines and wings. The cannons also changed shape, adjusting beams for range or damage as the pilot's needs changed.

The human's brown eyes were fixed on him.

"Bad juju," the human said flatly. "Ugly combination rage hunt your friends across Wildspace. You fix?"

Another shrug. He didn't have a nest here he could trust if violence was the only solution. And the death urges had long since burned themselves out.

"Not without finding my old nest and a few others," Glaxu said. "That new ship would be the sort of challenge they would look forward to, but I don't have the money to hire that many of my own killers to make a hunt out of it."

"Looking for other job now?" Ozzo asked. "Your name appears on winds of rumor this morning. Killer for hire, with own tiny gunship."

"Who started those rumors?" Glaxu let his voice get hard.

"Ah," the human nodded absently. "That make sense. You think Ex-wife? Play game?"

Bayjy and Leader had a high opinion of the merchant. Old connections that had served Miss Lavender in earlier visits.

"Do you know?" Glaxu asked bluntly.

Neither of them had made any motion towards the coin. Ozzo reached out now and grasped it in one, grizzled wingtip. He held it up, studying it for a moment as if it would speak to him.

"We put this to use and find out," he said quietly, sliding it into a pocket. "Have contact. Now, little killer, interest you in hand-held blades? Or whatever correct term is?"

Glaxu scoffed, but only internally. Mondi and human were both erect and bipedal, but that was about where the comparisons ended. Opposable thumb, but he couldn't make a true fist, like the tree shrews could, since his feathers got in the way. Holding a pistol involved pushing his middle finger or ring finger, to use the human terms, into the trigger guard. Those didn't have feathers like the pointer and pinky.

Trying to fight with a handheld blade was silly.

Especially with his short arms. He would use his much-longer legs and his dewclaw to fight. Had. They worked fine to kill humans and related creatures.

Still, Ozzo was being a friend today, so Glaxu could smile innocently and let the merchant work his spiel.

The device was one he was unfamiliar with, but it looked like something made for a Mondi hand. Thumb hole and finger hole that he could grasp, and keep as tight a grip as a human's paw could. Ten centimeters of blade, sharpened for about eight of them down both sides, with a tip that was a barely sharpened chisel coming to a point quickly from a heavy spine down the center.

"You hold," Ozzo handed it to him pommel first.

Glaxu did. The grip felt natural, which was unnatural this far from home. Perhaps it had been designed for a Mondi hand.

"Now, snap like whip," the merchant grinned.

Glaxu gave the human a sarcastic eyeroll, but stepped back from the counter to make some space, just because he had no idea what to expect.

He drew his wrist back and then flicked it forward, like a beak strike. He nearly dropped the weapon when it telescoped outward in a manner similar to Dave's baton, except that it retained the edges and returned to his fist quickly again, like a beak strike.

"You like?" Ozzo asked with a terrible, killing smile on his face.

"Where?" Glaxu sputtered.

The tiny human laughed and laughed and laughed, leaving Glaxu feeling rather like a fool.

"Is junk store," the man finally managed to get the gales of laughter under control. "Things arrive, come to rest, await need. Need arrives, often in the most unexpected shapes."

Glaxu turned the blade over in his hand and contemplated it. This wasn't anything he was familiar with among his kind, but he was a pilot, not a martial artist, and this had most likely been made by some evil Mondi who had obviously wanted a third dewclaw with which to strike.

"How much?" Glaxu asked, handing it back to the man, but he refused.

It ended up on the counter between them.

The human quoted an outrageous price.

"Seriously?" Glaxu scorned him.

"No, little killer friend," the human grinned. "Now we dicker."

[25]
BAYJY

SHE HAD BORROWED the book from Captain so she could read the entire thing in her cabin. Bayjy wasn't sure what she was looking for, but she suspected it was there. She would find it.

Valentinian had bought it on Kryuome from that weird dude Marduk, looking for some ancient maps he could use to compare geography against the coordinates from that silly-ass map he had won in that crooked poker game. Seriously, you couldn't make shit like this up, because nobody would believe it.

At least until you pulled out that map and showed it to them.

T'Ilard had been a regional palace, back then. The Urlan did things weird. Had, at least. Royal families tended to run into the thousands, because the cultural ideal of the big, dumb Urlan warrior meant one male frequently went for at least five sons and three daughters.

At least two of the males were expected to die off

at a young age doing stupid shit, but that just meant that the breeding stats generally evened out that way.

The more important the dude, the more kids he had. It got worse when you got into some of those bizarre religious sects that held that a successful male should have as many as fourteen wives.

Family reunions must have come with programs, just to list all the names and relations, so you could calculate if the cute boy you ran into was far enough away genetically to marry, and important enough across clan and tribal lines to make a good business arrangement for your family.

Wiping the Urlan Empire out really hadn't been that great a cultural setback, when you got right down to it.

But that still left her with T'Ilard.

Bayjy had printed out maps from the wall plotter, color-coded against overlays from the scanners. Levels of background radiation, like splotches of red paint that faded, the safer you got. They were tacked to the walls around her to keep her sharp.

Nowhere in this zone was safe, but as long as you showered regularly and didn't stay more than two months every few years, you weren't likely to get two-headed babies. Plus, they were doing things to their diet now that would help later, adding all manner of extras, however prophylactic they might be.

Someone had been angry when they hit this place with nuclear bombs. Accurate, too. The palace itself was a jumble of rock reduced to a small hill by the accumulation of two thousand winters of blowing grit. A couple of military bases were simply blood drops on the map, so intense even today that you didn't even want to spend too much time downwind.

And muties knew that. They had built a compound city out in what had been the lakebed, upwind. Bayjy wondered if that meant that they were smart enough to dig tunnels into the rich soil below them for clean dirt to grow things, since the surface stuff might glow on a really dark night in places.

They weren't supposed to be that smart, according to what the city folk had said, but she was beginning to assume some level of cultural chauvinism going on that nobody wanted to talk about.

And then the chapter about the city itself. The one that had set Vee off. Tourism guide as much as anything. Most of it was crap, but the references to the great map and how it held the treasure for the ages stored among the stars. Plain as print, if you understood Urlan culture, which few people did.

Urlan didn't do museums. Never had. It was a human thing to show off your wealth and prestige to commoners by collecting valuable cultural artifacts and charging an admission fee.

Urlan did palaces, where the exterior was grand and imposing, and lined the interior with all their gold and jewels. But you had to store shit. Hide it when you had more treasure than halls for it. Or stuff so priceless that you didn't even let the servants and slave species near it.

And those were underground vaults. Hidden. Bolt holes you could flee to if you faced an uprising of the lesser species. Like the whole, damned war had been.

On paper, there wasn't much to expect. Any

smart Urlan prince or princess would have evacuated their crap elsewhere, except that most of those folks had been evacuated to Kryuome ahead of other places being splattered by angry humans and all their cousins.

Kryuome was supposed to be a safe-behind-the-lines kind of place. Except that there weren't none of those when you had overdrives. Killer humans could just leapfrog to other worlds.

So the war had dropped out of warpbubbles and starting pelting the planet with big bombs. Dirty nukes. Suggestions of biological weapons, but Bayjy had read enough science to understand what stress and new germs from other planets could do all by themselves.

And then someone decided to hit the planet with something big enough to knock it slightly out of orbit. Not enough to destroy it, but it was closer to the local sun now than it had been. Drier as a result of all the natural and artificial heat introduced.

Must have had massive groundquakes for a damned long time before things stopped ringing. If they ever had.

That could be a problem when they got back there. Soil and rock probably had shifted around to the point that they couldn't open it up and find whatever was under that planet gem. Big Guy's muscles would come into play at that point. Or Kyrie and that big, sticking twin pulsar of her, worse come to worst.

Bayjy put the book down and looked around her cabin. Wouldn't be hers much longer. Plumbing and air were in place, back aft over the bay. Walls were going up next, to frame out a crew kitchen and rec room not that much different from what Vee and Dave had down and forward. More storage. Two oversized crew cabins for her and Kyrie to upgrade, and six more the same size as this one.

She wondered if they were wasting their time doing it. There was always a chance that someone had beat them to the punch. Twenty centuries was a long time for a secret to be kept. But if they were the first…

Any sort of big treasure would change things again. And she knew how much Valentinian disliked change, especially now, when he had finally gotten his head wrapped around making *Longshot Hypothesis* a place for a family, and not just a crew.

Would he buy a bigger ship? Or just trade at this scale, so he and some First Mate could go back to being wanderers? Would Big Guy stay, or buy himself a new identity and retire to a beach somewhere? Would Kyrie do the same?

What did you do, if you suddenly had access to wealth beyond imagination?

Butler would have probably managed to blow it all in less than five years, living like a pig and forgetting about tomorrow until he couldn't afford lunch one day.

And were they a bigger target as a team, where people might recognize a group description? Or could they vanish into the trillions of beings out there, not just in Wildspace, but those places where the Dominion folk had come from? That was only one of six sides of Wildspace. The Mondi were another, from what Glaxu had said.

That left four.

What did she want from her life? Bayjy had

closed the book, so she rested her hand on the fabric-covered cover now, as if she could absorb the wisdom of the ages from it by osmosis.

She had no home. Just a series of stations and ships she had been on all her life, even back before she had run off to get rich. No family she had seen in more than a decade. That happened in space. You had to be self-contained.

Salvaging was a thing she was good at. Three dimensional problem solving to make the fewest cuts in the fastest time, so you could show the best profit when you got the loot back to whatever fixer, fence, or factor was interested.

Even that haul from the Urlan troop transport wouldn't have done more than set her up for a few years of goofing off, or let her invest in a couple of retirement schemes for later.

Did she even want to retire? Thirty-three Standard was too young to consider that, even if she got lucky and rich. Too many years ahead of her that needed to be insured against, in a galaxy that really didn't believe in giving a girl an even break.

No, the best thing that had ever happened to her was wandering into that poker game with Vee and the others. Opportunity, if you could grab it and hold on.

Look where it had gotten her. Poised on the verge of…something.

Bayjy wasn't sure, but there was so much nobody really knew.

What would Glaxu bring back to the fire? How safe was it to return to Kryuome, as opposed to bouncing off to someplace like Vorcia Thiri?

Trade was right out. She understood that.

Longshot Hypothesis could get a reputation as a fast, honest ship, that was sure, but the Widow would hear. Would come running and gunning. If she could.

Nobody gave Glaxu credit. He might have arranged an accident or just attacked the Widow, if he thought he could score a quick kill and get away afterwards. Mean, dangerous, little ground cuckoo.

Bayjy set the book on the bunk and stood up. She'd been too deep in it and herself. She needed something to help her calm down so she could sleep.

They were on the verge of something. Maybe the greatest discovery in centuries.

And maybe Dave's wife coming out of warp right on top of them, guns blazing.

[26]

GLAXU

GLAXU WAS FEELING proud of himself. Leader had told stories about the grand negotiations with a book dealer, of all people, in Meeredge, even greater than subsequent battles with the being's cousin over something as mundane as guns.

This last hour had netted him nothing more interesting than a knife-whip meant for Mondi hands, but he had gotten the feeling that Ozzo had come away equally impressed. At least he would respect the abilities of the next Mondi that came along.

The knife-whip was secured in his bandolier for now. The human merchant had possessed nothing like a proper sheath for it, whatever that might look like, so it was in a pouch until he could get back to the ship and putter.

There was a most flamboyant rhythm to his stride as he walked.

Right up until the moment he came around that

last corner and saw what was waiting for him. Or rather, whom.

Glaxu had expected the Widow to keep Butler Vidy-Wooders on a shorter leash. Probably, she had intended to, and gotten distracted by some political machinations along the way.

Didn't matter all that much. The M'Rai was here. Not exactly guarding the lock to *Outermost*, but making it plain that Glaxu would have to deal with him and the two humans with him, if he wished to board.

He supposed running was an option. Technically, it always was, when one was faced with overwhelming odds.

Glaxu didn't really think that two human punks and a M'Rai qualified in that department. Maybe if any of them had actually appeared dangerous, but the two humans were standing around like witnesses at a car wreck, and Vidy-Wooders was apparently drunk enough to do something stupid. More stupid than normal.

Even from here, the smell of alcohol was intense enough that Glaxu wondered if the creature was trying to poison land mollusks with his breath.

Glaxu took it all in and slowed from his normal jaunt to a careful walk. Nobody was holding any sort of ranged weapon right now, so it wasn't just an ambush, however stupidly Glaxu had just walked into one, not paying attention.

"Hey, bird man," the M'Rai called in a drunken snarl. "Been waiting for you."

"You're not my type, tree shrew," Glaxu cat-called back. "I prefer mates with a three-digit IQ."

At least one of the humans was sober enough to

catch the multi-layered insult. That one staggered a little more upright and started to say something, but Bayjy's old captain called him off.

"Enough," Vidy-Wooders snarled. "You're making me look bad, roadrunner."

"I'm sorry," Glaxu sneered at the creature. "I wasn't aware you needed help with that."

M'Rai were stupid creatures. Bullies, Miss Lavender had said on more than one occasion. Engineered originally for mass and muscle, and not much brains. This one must have been an archetype. Or maybe he just represented the lower half of the scale.

But his skin was too thin. Probably too much alcohol had sanded all his dermal armor off, or whatever human variants did to engage in verbal fisticuffs.

"Blond lady sees you, and thinks maybe she doesn't need me so much," the man snarled, taking a step forward. "Maybe hires you instead and old Butler's out on his ass."

"Oh, I doubt she's that intelligent," Glaxu taunted the creature, edging slightly to his left. "Women like her always need your kind."

Whatever kind that was.

This corridor was down in the cheap zones of the outer ring of the station. A spur off that, even, sticking out like a single finger so that ships that didn't need to get in and out of dock all that often could be packed relatively close together. Freighters needed more free volume, coming and going, and they paid a premium for it. *Outermost* was just another runabout. With guns.

If the M'Rai moved too quickly, Glaxu could take

one long stride to the side from here. That put a bench and planter box in the way, the latter sucking up carbon dioxide and other pollutants while putting out clean oxygen.

Options, depending on the weapon he decided to use here.

"My kind?" the M'Rai's rage slid a little to the side as his confusion woke up. He stopped moving, which was to his benefit. "What's that supposed to mean?"

"Mindless violence," Glaxu said. "Full frontal assault on a defended hardpoint. Sometimes that's the only solution, so it's handy to have folks who think that's a smart idea."

"I don't think she needs you," Vidy-Wooders growled, eyes moving and hand clenching, but otherwise still.

None of them had holsters visible. Might not mean they were unarmed. Maybe, like Glaxu, they had something tucked under an arm where it took just a shade longer to get to it.

For now, nobody had a gun out though, so it could be that the beast just wanted to issue a warning. That he needed to bring a pair of drinking buddies either meant he wanted witnesses, or maybe he unconsciously realized that he was already out of his depth against one Mondi slayership pilot.

"So convince her not to hire me," Glaxu mocked the man. "I've got other gigs on the boards I could pursue."

However stupid and inane they might be, but he didn't say that out loud.

"I think you're a spy."

The M'Rai did take a step forward now.

Just one.

Glaxu decided that the man had finally worked himself up to violence. Some folks had to walk a long path before they had the courage to provoke a confrontation. Alcohol apparently helped among humans, as did certain recreational substances ingested via other means.

Butler Vidy-Wooders wasn't just a dumb bully, but not by much. Still, there was truth to his observation. Glaxu was a spy.

He wondered if he would have to kill the M'Rai now, just to keep the man from throwing a tantrum of accusations in front of the Widow. Wouldn't matter if she believed. The seed would have been planted. At some point, it would sprout, and perhaps bloom.

Dave had shared a few stories about life in the inner reaches of the Dominion. The rampant paranoia and constant misdirections and maneuvering for face and status. Right now, the Widow considered her pet Mondi as just another thug to be triple-crossed at some point.

Glaxu was still a little insulted at such a low number.

If you're going to do something, madam, I would have appreciated five or more layers of deception. Something worth getting out of my cactus for.

Glaxu let his eyes turn cold and angry on the M'Rai.

"And I think you're an amateur punk," he snapped back at the giant. "The only thing you bring are your mating proclivities, however warped and disgusting you'll need to get to remain in her bed."

He liked the way the monster's eyes flared a little.

Took Vidy-Wooders nearly two seconds to process that through the alcohol and overall mental torpor.

"I'll kill you," the M'Rai snarled and took an enormous stride forward.

Humans liked to get themselves out-flanked by other creatures, because they don't take relative size into account. Mondi rarely fought something their own size that wasn't another Mondi, so they were used to dealing with oversized creatures with commensurate egos.

Three meters tall. Nine feet to use the other human measure. Triple his size. Probably nine times his mass.

Big, dumb, AND slow.

Butler Vidy-Wooders stepped up onto the bench, and then into the planter, apparently intent on pouncing on a tiny ground cuckoo like a skytiger.

Glaxu wasn't there. And he even waited until the M'Rai took the step up and jumped before he moved.

Three-on-one wasn't even a remotely fair fight, but Glaxu didn't want the other two having time to call in some friends. He raced at the nearer one and kicked at the human's ankle hard with torque and speed as he went by. This creature also outweighed him, probably by a factor of about five, but he was standing wrong, and not all that sober.

Losing a leg caused him to face-plant with a yelp that ended in the bong of a head impacting deck surprisingly fast.

Glaxu hadn't paused long enough to see it. He was onto the second human with two strides.

Maybe he was showing off. Just a little. Take the momentum and leap, letting your mass carry you past your bewildered dipshit of a target at his head level, so his eyes are just starting to turn when you draw a dewclaw across his face.

Not the dewclaw today, because Valentinian had insisted on shock bracers. With good reason. Butler Vidy-Wooders had indeed started this, security recordings of the incident would confirm that.

But this particular human had done nothing to warrant lethal force. At least not yet.

Glaxu wasn't interested in finding out what these two could do that would require such a hostile response, so he was taking them both down in a most civilized manner.

Pre-Meditated Self-Defense, as Leader had described it.

One shock bracer to the side of the head, right where humans apparently have a significant collection of nerve endings, right behind and below the ear itself.

One arc of electricity later, and the second human was down.

Butler Vidy-Wooders was just getting himself turned around from where his stupid leap had taken him.

"You think you're cute, bird?" the tree shrew snarled as he started back this direction.

"You could go whimpering back to the Widow," Glaxu snapped, goading the shit some more. "I promise not to embarrass you too much in public, as long as you behave like a proper, little lapdog."

My my my. Sensitive spot, Captain?

Glaxu considered just shooting him right now. He hadn't brought along a pistol powerful enough to kill a M'Rai outright, unlike Valentinian or Kyriaki did when on station these days. Still, the little popgun in his holster would probably stun the monster long enough for Glaxu to do nasty things to him.

And he felt the need.

But again, self-defense.

I couldn't run, officer. He was so big that he would just chase me down and squish me.

No, best to wait for the drunkard to escalate things. Hopefully, no innocent civilians would have the unluck to be needing this corridor in the next few minutes.

Glaxu checked the floor around him. Mostly clear, save for he and his opponent, plus that bench and planter. Both other humans down, although the first one was rolling himself over, or trying to. Blood seemed to be leaking from his face.

Apparently human noses were more fragile than Mondi beaks.

He made a note to stay away from the slippery spots on the floor where the blood was dripping. He was already uncomfortable fighting on steel decks, rather than the wood ones he had in *Outermost*. Wearing these boots in public was a painful fashion failure, however necessary it might be.

But you had to do these things when you might need to maneuver rapidly.

Vidy-Wooders went for a pocket and Glaxu nearly drew his pistol right then, except that the man came out with what looked for all the world like a rigid snake made of black leather.

Ah. Sap. A human weapon. Easy to manufacture. Generally considered nonlethal under most legal systems. Still deadly in the hands of a raging M'Rai.

Vidy-Wooders flicked it back and forth in his right hand.

"Wanna dance fancy for me, little bird?" the giant taunted, advancing slowly.

Glaxu rotated to his left again, rather than merely give ground. Doing that would eventually put his tail feathers up against the bulkhead at the end of the corridor with the big portal to watch ships sailing into and out of dock.

"Can you even dance, ox?" Glaxu fired back. "I thought you were just a dumb thug with a big mouth."

The M'Rai charged, hand out to one side with that snake all set to bite or sweep.

Glaxu didn't bother doing anything except scampering off to one side, letting the brute cut the chord of his circle while shifting away.

Making your opponent angry is a good thing, if it makes them sloppy. Vidy-Wooders didn't have that mad gleam in his eyes right now.

No, he looked suddenly sober, as if everything up until now had been a ruse. Either that or he was a high-functioning drunkard who could still fight inebriated.

Glaxu didn't wish to find out. At this point, the security tapes would show him defending himself without attacking, save for the two fools on the deck.

Vidy-Wooders waved the snake at him again. It was all Glaxu could do not to take a bite at it, but he doubted the M'Rai understood that he was technically offering the Mondi a late lunch.

"Come fight me," the giant bellowed, stepping forward and swinging overhead.

Glaxu slipped the blow by stepping back, glancing around just enough to confirm how close to the wall he had gotten. He exploded sideways and raced to the center of the corridor as the giant turned.

"Go home, amateur hour," Glaxu snarled. "Leave the fighting for experts."

Oooh. Another chink in the big man's armor. Must have all sorts of adequacy issues tucked up in there. Wonder what a competent psychologist might make of him, given six months and an unlimited therapy budget.

Vidy-Wooders began to stalk now, howling with indignation and holding his hands out as far to his sides as they could go.

Glaxu wished he could grin in the human manner right now, just to taunt the beast silently. Being only a meter tall, he could slide right under those hands unless the giant got almost down on his knees, which would end this fight pretty damned quick.

The beast charged again.

Glaxu cursed himself silently, as a boot as big as he was just missed connecting with his arm as he moved away. He had been thinking of the tree shrews as handsy creatures, forgetting that they could also kick.

If one of those feet connected, Glaxu was pretty sure he'd have a broken leg or head.

He had had about enough of this shit.

One wing went to the bandolier and brought out the new knife-whip. It looked even less dangerous in his hands than the pistol did.

He moved backwards a safe distance and squared up on the giant humanling.

"Last warning, Butler Vidy-Wooders," Glaxu called out in a nice, clean enunciation that even low-budget security systems ought to be able to record cleanly. "Go away or I will hurt you."

"You can't hurt anything, roadrunner," the M'Rai snarled back and began to stalk closer.

Technically, the M'Rai captain hadn't been there on Kryuome, when Glaxu had decided that he had had enough of that particular taunt. Too many of Truqtok's people had latched onto it as a way to bait the Mondi.

After three of them ended up dead, the remainder had learned to keep more civil tongues in their mouths.

Still, he had promised to kill the next shell-less bastard who called him that. Looked like maybe it was Butler Vidy-Wooders's lucky day.

Or something like that.

Glaxu remained perfectly still as the man closed. Again, it was a shame that he couldn't grin in a way that the M'Rai might appreciate. Bayjy had told him that a Mondi grin looked more like a constipated weasel than anything.

The failures of cross-species nonverbal communications.

Mondi did growl. Louder than a feline purring. Less than a canine showing anger.

But the corridor was quite empty and rather quiet at the moment.

Mondi growls and M'Rai footsteps.

Glaxu watched the beast's eyes and his center of gravity, so badly off for having to engage such a compact, speedy target.

The hands gave it all away. Glaxu watched the muscles telegraph the attack.

The sap came overhead, but intentionally wide, the goal to force him to remain in the center instead of floating to his left again like he preferred. Lining him up for another kick.

One mighty boot reared back like a cobra trying to scare someone off. It started forward, but at a rate that cobras would have been embarrassed by.

Glaxu exploded into motion to his right, just enough to plant his outer two toes, then he pushed back to his left as he moved forward.

The big, leather boot, underpolished but probably black when it left the factory originally, passed by his back so slowly he brushed his tail feathers against it, crossing in between the M'Rai's legs and landing his hop just behind the stupid tree shrew.

The knife-whip had never been blooded in his possession. Fitting, since he had only owned it for an hour.

Time to remedy that.

Hop to the left foot and plant to kill inertia. Compact everything like a snake about to leap into space. Snap the right arm out and across a horizon with the wrist pinions. Rotate on the shoulders, the hips, and the left ankle for torque.

Head comes around faster than the arm, so you can spot the blow. Your target is three ugly meters tall, scaled proportionally to a human like Valentinian Tarasicodissa. He is wearing boots that come nearly to his knees, front and back.

Nearly was the key.

Wasn't it always?

Glaxu watched the extended edge, out near the weight that pulled the blade taut, enter the back of Butler Vidy-Wooder's knee, just below the hinge point.

There was no blood yet. No pain either, as the nerves were limited by chemistry.

Glaxu finished his rotation, a miniature dust devil coming to rest on the deck with one hand out. Because he was angry, he hopped onto his right foot, slashing outwards with the left and letting the shock bracer add a bit of electrical overload to the signals racing madly up the monster's spine to tell his brain that he was suddenly in a great deal of trouble.

Butler Vidy-Wooders tried to turn around, and discovered that one of his legs didn't work anymore. He collapsed instead, falling onto his side and then his back.

Glaxu figured that if he didn't do it now, he'd have to fight this stupid bastard again, and the moron would probably bring enough friends next time, if he ever got out of a lifterchair.

Did the Widow need this punk enough to have an expensive doctor repair that level of damage?

Glaxu decided not to find out. He could always claim that his training had taken over and he was running on autopilot right now. Whether station security would buy it was a different story for a different day, but it would hopefully look reasonable.

He hopped into the air and snapped the knife-whip again, this time cutting a deep gash right across the M'Rai's throat, nearly to the spine.

He landed, blowing air heavily as the adrenaline lit a fire in his belly and under his ass.

One more jolt with the shock bracer, holding it against the flesh for long enough that the human was out cold and would never wake up again.

Redtip Windrunner Oedressa *Farther* Glaxu hopped backwards and surveyed his work, collapsed knife-whip describing a compact figure eight in his right hand as he turned to track the humans. One was out cold, and would remain that way for a few more minutes.

The other had managed to crawl as far backwards as a handy bulkhead, where the cold, impersonal steel had stopped him, much as he wanted to keep backing away. Red blood drained from the human's nostrils and stained his face and his clothing, but the eyes were only vaguely human right now.

They grew enormous as Glaxu locked eyes on him and started to advance. Strange sounds emanated from the creature's mouth.

Signs of panic, Glaxu assumed.

He pointed at Butler Vidy-Wooders with the knife-whip, watching the human's eyes mindlessly follow.

"You will tell the authorities that it was his idea," Glaxu stated clearly, the anger in his voice evident. "He started it. He decided to attack one Mondi and you went along with it. It was all his fault. Otherwise, I'll come for you next."

The smell of ammonia joined the harsh copper of the blood. The man had just pissed himself in fear.

Well, that was a new one.

"Am I understood?" Glaxu demanded in a voice that not-Dave-Hall might have used.

The man seemed incapable of rational vocabulary, but nodded like a shaken rag doll.

Glaxu decided that he could not ask for much more, and this could be the only chance he had to get away from station firepower, depending on how specist the bastards were.

He approached the lock and keyed it open, using

his card-reader to unlock the secondary systems that would keep out any but the most capable burglars.

Inside, he locked everything twice and hurried to the cockpit. Food could wait until he was away, regardless of how hungry he was.

The death of Butler Vidy-Wooders would make the galaxy a better place, of that Glaxu had no doubts, but he didn't know how it would impact the Widow's mission. Hopefully, she was too far along with her new ship to back out now and buy something neither he nor Leader would see coming.

But Glaxu could not think of a better way to inject chaos right now.

She might realize he was a spy, but she might do that anyway, him having killed her pet M'Rai, even in a duel. This way, the truth would never been known. Not for sure.

If she hired a more competent pilot, she might do better, but without Vidy-Wooders or Redtip, she would be back to her starting point.

He would buy Valentinian time to make use of this intelligence.

"Chatosig-Six Flight Control, this is Mondi slayership *Outermost*, requesting a lane assignment for outbound flight," he said into the radio as he raced through his pre-flight.

Glaxu held his breath as he waited.

If Security had seen the carnage on their cameras, they could just lock his ship down tight now and knock politely at his rear airlock.

It would be polite, the first time. They were like that.

Four big bolts retracted with hollow thumps and Glaxu found that he could breathe again.

"Outbound lane two five three, level four assigned, *Outermost*," a woman's voice came over the line. "Safe flight."

"And you," he replied, killing the line and bringing the nose of his ship around. Like *Longshot Hypothesis*, *Outermost* backed into a station and could fly directly away, without vectoring around on thrusters like most ships.

What fool had thought up that silly of an architecture, anyway?

Engines live, he brought power to the wings, keeping the geometry compact and streamlined. There was no atmosphere up here, but being small would make him hard to hit, if someone opened fire.

Time to get gone.

[27]
ATHANASIA

TECHNICALLY, the idiot was not yet one of her employees, but Athanasia supposed that Station Security was right in the assumptions they were willing to make. Butler Vidy-Wooders had sold *Hard Bargain* and salted the funds into a bank.

She wondered if the M'Rai had any next of kin that had a claim on the funds, the kind of thing that financial facilities required on their paperwork in the Dominion. Out here, it was probably a much less orderly state in banking as well. They would declare him dead, wait a year, and probably claim all the cash.

Athanasia made a mental note to see if she could come up with a way to bribe the authorities here. Maybe a signed investment agreement giving the man a share in her vessel for some amount of cash. If she was willing to take a third, they might be willing to let it slide and make the rest just vanish.

She knew how accountants worked.

"Is that all you have?" she asked as the recording

finished and she was again looking at the face of the head of Station Security.

"That is correct, Ambassador," the woman said.

At least they had decided to honor her Dominion rank, even way the hell across Wildspace. Perhaps it lent the station a bit of importance.

Or something.

"We will need some time to make arrangements here," Athanasia went ahead with her bluff. "Paperwork had been signed but not yet filed, as we worked out the correct authorities to handle things. Butler Vidy-Wooders was to be hired on as our Pilot as part of the partnership that was taking place."

"As long as you take your new plaything elsewhere and remain polite, we won't have any issues sorting things out here," the woman said in a way that finessed one of the most polite threats Athanasia had seen from the locals.

Take your new warship and go play pirate somewhere else. Don't bring your troubles onto my station, any more than you already have. Pay cash up front.

Athanasia understood those lines, and was willing to work within them for now. *Dominion-427* was just about ready to back away from the station, minus more than a third of its original crew, and make the long run for Cronus Prime, bearing notice to the relevant parties that Athanasia had chosen to remain well and away from Dominion space.

She wouldn't ever return. So be it.

Losing Vidy-Wooders just meant that she had to hire another pilot who understood Wildspace, one she didn't have nearly as good a hold on as she had done with the M'Rai.

Redtip would have been acceptable, but she could understand him fleeing. The Mondi wouldn't, couldn't be sure she hadn't set the giant on him, either as a test or just to eliminate all options.

Redtip fleeing neither implicated him nor exonerated the creature. She might see him again at another station, and might not. If she did, the only relevant question would be if anyone had seen Valentinian Tarasicodissa or the man calling himself Dave Hall,

Or that little bitch of a renegade cop, Kyriaki Apokapes. Athanasia still had a score to settle there, as well.

Still, in a tenday or so, she would have enough firepower to do pretty much anything she chose, short of starting a war with one of the few multi-systemic empires and republics that had clawed their way out of the primordial slime of Wildspace and last longer than a generation.

The M'Rai pirates had done a reasonable job of breaking the last major political force around here fifty-five years ago, and in the process necessitating eventually putting this ship on blocks until someone else could afford to put it back into commission.

It would rise again, like the bird of legend that was consumed in the fires, born again, and return to conquer. Rather like Athanasia.

She was looking forward to going hunting for *Longshot Hypothesis* aboard her own *Phoenix*.

[28]

VALENTINIAN

For once, Valentinian was glad that nobody really felt the need to get wildly experimental in the kitchen, most of the time. Pull something from the freezerbox, run it through the microwave for the correct number of seconds listed on the cover, peel the top, and serve.

His stomach really didn't need spicy and exotic right now.

"You're sure?" he asked as Glaxu finished his tale.

"Which part?" the Mondi replied, cocking his head left and then right, like he did when rolling his eyes at someone might seem rude.

"Oh, I assume Butler's a corpse," Valentinian laughed. "And good riddance. Probably be worth bribing someone one of these days, if they kept a copy of that fight for their records."

"They will," Bayjy spoke up with a grim laugh. "Every time there is a death they have to keep a copy for ten years, in case there's a lawsuit later."

"So what is the problem, then, Valentinian?" Glaxu asked.

"How the hell do we deal with something like what she's building for herself?" Valentinian asked. "Dave, you got any ideas?"

"Run like hell," the Big Guy offered. "She's already looking beyond revenge at this point. That's enough firepower to build her own gang or capture some planet and set herself up for life."

"And running helps?" Valentinian turned to face him squarely now, pausing only to glance at Kyriaki and see if she had anything to contribute. "While she becomes a pirate queen?"

"It does, actually," Kyriaki put down her soup and popped her neck once. "Ties her down to a physical location. Limits her reach, at least as far as she had to offer bigger bribes to get people to come after us, since she can't just chase us if we don't want to stay put."

"Is there anything that can stop that ship?" Valentinian looked at each of them in turn.

"My old nest, plus three more like it, would suffer serious casualties in the process of killing her vessel, unless we managed surprise," Glaxu said calmly.

"A Dominion Shield could mess with her quite nicely," Dave laughed. "To say nothing of a ZoneStriker. Doubt I'd be able to order someone to chase her down these days."

The others laughed. It released some of the tension that had built up.

"So what do we do?" Valentinian asked.

He was aware that it would be his decision, but they were committing their own lives if he screwed up, so they needed to be able to be heard.

"Been thinking about options, Vee," Bayjy spoke quietly.

He turned to her and nodded.

"So we don't want to head back in the Dominion direction," Bayjy said. "Laurentia might just welcome her back, but not if she decided to carve out an empire of her own instead of helping fight Dave's old friends."

He agreed with that sentiment. So did the others. And the Widow would never settle for being a servant, that much was clear.

"Other direction, we've got the sectors where you would find more Mondi nests out being all piratical, like Glaxu here was before," Bayjy nodded.

Valentinian caught the nod from the Mondi.

"But that leaves us two huge arcs of space to get lost in," she continued. "Upstream or downstream, depending. We go out one of those and she likely never finds us again, especially if she wants to start her own empire around here."

"Does she have to stay local?" Kyriaki asked. "Your old captain knew these regions, but with him dead, any place is as good as anywhere else. She could just pick a direction as well."

"Then we're playing whack-a-mole, trying to outguess her," Dave chimed in. "I have no great preference which way we go, as long as it escapes her and my old gang at the same time."

"Me, too," Kyriaki added.

Valentinian looked at Bayjy and noted the shadow in the back of her eyes.

"But?" he prompted her.

"I got a gut feeling, Vee," she said. "It's still there,

under the radioactive sands of Kryuome, whatever it was they put down so long ago."

"And there's the risk, isn't it?" he replied. "The one place the Widow might choose to look for us."

"That thing's the size of a Dominion Poniard," Dave said fiercely. "No way in hell it can land on a planetary surface. Probably had a permanent cargo shuttle or two on blisters, or in one of those boxes Glaxu described. Just because they couldn't fit *Outermost* doesn't mean that they can't get to the surface. But that monster has to stay in space. Gives us options to run, if she shows up while we're there."

"So two votes for Kryuome," Valentinian said. "Glaxu? Kyriaki?"

"I didn't kill that M'Rai just to turn around and get cold feet for Dave's wife," Glaxu huffed with a laugh. "Let us dig."

"Rich would be nice," Kyriaki added.

Valentinian nodded to them, and then himself. It was his ship, at the end of the day. They had chosen to have him as their captain, in charge of their lives, when any of them could have gone elsewhere along the way.

On the one hand, the bad luck to draw the Widow in her new warship, all set to conquer known space. Stacked against it, the chance that they would open an empty hole in the ground, just as the T'Brask muties came rampaging over the hill to kill the infidels that had defiled their holy land.

On the other hand, just the slightest chance of finding true treasure. *Screw you money*, as his dad had always called it.

The odds were somewhere right up there with drawing a Perfect Arcade on the seventh card.

But he was a gambler. Always had been. Dave had accused him of being able to fall into shit and come out smelling like roses.

Time to put that to the test.

"Pack your hats and suntan lotion, ladies and gentlemen," his smile seemed infectious, mirrored in the other faces. "Looks like we're going to the desert."

READ MORE!

Be sure to read all of the Shadow of the Dominion books!

Longshot Hypothesis
Hard Bargain
Outermost
Dominion-427
Phoenix
Princess Rualoh

Web: www.blazeward.com
Boundary Shock Quarterly (BSQ):
https://www.boundaryshockquarterly.com/

facebook.com/KRPBlaze

goodreads.com/Blaze_Ward

bookbub.com/authors/blaze-ward

Knotted Road Press fiction specializes in dynamic writing set in mysterious, exotic locations.

Knotted Road Press non-fiction publishes autobiographies, business books, cookbooks, and how-to books with unique voices.

Knotted Road Press creates DRM-free ebooks as well as high-quality print books for readers around the world.

With authors in a variety of genres including literary, poetry, mystery, fantasy, and science fiction, Knotted Road Press has something for everyone.

Knotted Road Press
www.KnottedRoadPress.com